Cameron

*"To Linda, for your Herculean patience
and depth of encouragement."*

Dennis

*"To the Master Story Teller,
for reaching hearts through parables."*

DO OR DIE TIME

DO OR DIE TIME

Cameron Ventura and Dennis Mansfield

Hidden Shelf Publishing House
P.O. Box 4168, McCall, ID 83638
www.hiddenshelfbooks.com

Graphic design: Allison Kaukola

Interior layout: Sarah Harris

Cover art: Cameron Ventura

Library of Congress Cataloguing-in-Publication Data

Ventura, Cameron and Mansfield, Dennis
Do or Die Time

ISBN: 0999646601
ISBN-13: 978-0999646601

Printed in the United States of America

Table of Contents

◊ CHAPTER 1 ◊

The Prune-Faced Hobo

Stumbling upon a grubby pair of legs, tucked in the maples like they were stashed purposefully, isn't a casual thing. It's not something a guy can just ride on past and shrug off like a dead cat in the alley. No sir, this is the kind of thing kids make up to scare the whiz outta other kids when they're camping out or sleeping over. So when James noticed the boots, and then the legs, we nearly crashed into each other stopping our bikes. We both stood stone-still . . . just staring.

"If that fella's sleeping," I said in my softest whisper, "he's gonna wake up with a serious case of the tingles with his leg jacked over like that."

That's what Gramps always called 'em—the tingles—when he'd wake up from an odd position and his hands or feet would get that sparkly feeling.

"Feels like a thousand little ants nibblin' on my fingers," he'd complain.

One of the legs sticking out of the maples was twisted

over in a way not intended by God. It looked like a ragdoll, thrown into the trash. The rest of the body was hid among the golden leaves, so we couldn't right off tell what was up with this fellow. The uncomfortable way he was resting made me start to wonder about his eternal condition. That's what Gram says when someone's passed over to the next life.

"That just doesn't look comfortable," I said, real low.

"It don't look comfortable at all," James whispered back, without taking his eyes off the legs. "Waddya think? I think he's dead . . . that's what I think. Wadda you think, Cal?"

Well, that's pretty much what I was starting to think too. And, let's get the heck outta here! The truth is, James didn't really care what I thought. I knew pretty quick that he was gonna want to mess around with whoever it was. James was like that when it came to creepy stuff. Not me.

I'll be honest, if those stumps even moved a muscle, I know for sure I'd be half way home before you could say Pronto Pups on a wooden stick. But they didn't, at least not yet.

"He might be asleep," I hoped. "My Uncle Phil got whacked with a hardball when he was a kid and it laid him up for half a day."

"Nah, I don't think he's asleep," James said softly. He mustered up his usual gumption and laid his bike down and walked a little closer. The dry leaves under his feet sounded suddenly very loud and crunchy.

"Mister?" James inquired at about normal volume. There was no answer . . . not even a flinch.

"Don't get too close," I said real soft. "He might come to and grab ya."

If that was the body's plan, I didn't want it to hear that I was on to it. The possibility of the body grabbing one of us suddenly did not seem all that crazy to me, not with a pair of legs poking out of the bushes like bait for curious kids.

Now, I was pretty sure that dead people don't jump up. Only in monster movies does that happen. But I'm not an expert, not like Martin Shift's uncle who runs the funeral home in Salmon. Besides, the only dead person I'd ever seen in my thirteen years was Gramps, and he didn't do any jumpin' around, or anything spooky at his funeral. But, like I said, I'm not experienced with the deceased. Only dead animals, and not all that many of them either.

All of a sudden though, I started thinking about Martin Swift's uncle, and the funeral home, and the stories that Marty'd told us while camping out in the back yard. I don't want to scare you, but those stories pretty much took the fun outta sleeping out for the rest of that summer.

Truth is, and if you tell anyone about this, well, I won't tell you anything more . . . I slept with a flashlight for a while after that. I'm not proud of it, but I wasn't takin' any chances.

So, I felt it my duty to make sure that James was at least aware of the possibility that something outta the ordinary could happen right about now. Something that might make even James sleep with a flashlight.

He must have been having similar thoughts, cuz he stood cocked and ready to jump as he gave one of the shabby boots a little kick. It just flopped back and forth and stopped still.

I was so scared that I was sure my legs had turned to rubber. Maybe I wouldn't even be able to run if the body decided to jump up. I'd look just like the scarecrow in the *Wizard of Oz* movie, fumbling around, falling down, flopping on the ground like a fish on the shore. In the meantime, that dead guy would be all over me, mauling and drooling and laughing a scary laugh as he killed me!

But, when I saw James relax, I started to breathe a little more normal too.

"I don't think he's asleep, Cal," he concluded after nothing happened from the "boot kick" test. "He's deader 'n a doornail."

James moved around to investigate further.

* * *

As much as James and me were pals and did most everything together, he was always the one taking the lead. James was taller, stronger, braver, and generally cooler than I ever would be. He even wore his hair long when the rest of us had crew cuts.

I tried to get Gram to let me grow out my bright red peach fuzz, hoping it would make a difference. She wouldn't. Besides, I doubt it would have made me any cooler. And James' usual gumption is what had him right now motion for me to follow as he inched closer to the body.

I got off my bike, but chose to maintain my distance, at least for the time being. I slumped down on a stump and watched, still not convinced this was at all a good idea.

It's the same reason I was squirmy at Gramps' funeral. Those stories Marty told us in the backyard started playing in my head while sitting there in the front row. I would have never sat that close to the front, but Dad had insisted we pay our respects, and get real close while we did it. What had worried me was the known fact that Gramps was a serious jokester, and I wasn't keen on him jumpin' up and doin' one of his tickle jobs on me at the funeral.

I didn't want to look at him either and was glad the box was closed up. But, when the prune-faced man with the twitchy eye came over and opened the coffin, I couldn't take my eyes off Gramps' stone-still face. My cousin Todd had to nudge me.

"You can blink, Cal," Todd had whispered seriously. "If he jumps out, or does anything weird while your eyes're closed, I'll let you know."

Even though Todd was a year older, he also wasn't so sure about dead bodies and their unpredictable tendencies.

It was just the same right now. I wasn't too keen on gettin' a closer look at whoever that was stashed in the shrubs, and couldn't turn and run either. That'd stick to me for the rest of my life that I, Cal Poag, ran from a dead man . . . who wasn't even chasin' me!

"Wadda we gonna do?" I asked, eager to hand off this weighty responsibility.

"Not sure just yet. But he's dead, so we got lots 'a time ta figure somethin'," James answered. I could see that he was getting more and more excited for the challenge.

"That's what I was afraid of," I groaned.

"Wadda ya mean by that? You think this kind of thing happens every day?"

"No . . ."

"Well then, get your chicken butt over here and help me."

"Help you what? I ain't touchin' that dead guy."

"Why? You think he's gonna bite ya?"

I just shrugged. I wasn't so sure yet. Maybe.

"This is a mystery, Calvin, so let's figure out what happened."

Calvin. I hated being called Calvin, and when James called me by my full name it generally meant trouble.

"I don't care what happened, James."

"Well, I'm lookin'," he said with that irritated tone aimed at egging me on, like I was going to be left out.

* * *

Maybe I should back up a bit so you can see just how we got here . . . staring at a pair of mangy pants and boots.

If you haven't figured it out yet, my name's Calvin Poag and James Nelson is my best friend. We spend nearly every day through the summer, and sometimes winter too, tramping around Mud Lake. That's where we live—Mud Lake, Washington.

I am not lying if I tell you that a week doesn't go by where we're not in some kind a jam. But we always get out of it. Well, almost always.

Anyway, unlike me, James hates fishing.

"It's just boring! We're just sitting, waiting for something to happen. I say we make something happen," he said with a grin. That's when he pulled a stick of dynamite out of his coat pocket. I was instantly sorry I'd mentioned the National Geographic story about some scientists blasting piranha in the Amazon so they could count them.

When the dynamite went off, I almost fell off the dock. When I got myself right-side-up, I realized it was like I was under a thick blanket. I couldn't hardly hear anything.

"You just blasted my ears off," I felt my mouth say, but I couldn't hear any words. Whatever he said back, all I saw was his mouth moving. His ears were obviously affected too, because he turned away from me and pointed at the water. That's when I saw those "lunker trout" slowly drift to the surface of Mosquito Lake's dark blue water. I was sure James would now be blasting fish at every one of my favorite fishing holes.

Whatever plans we had for collecting all those fish were suddenly cut short when the thick bushes by the water's edge started to move. Someone had heard the blast and was coming to investigate.

James grabbed my arm and spun me around and we scrambled off the dock and into some brambles. We got hid just before two men appeared at the water's edge, looking around for what had just blown up. One was huge with a giant head that sat on his wide slumping shoulders. The other much smaller and skinny. My attention kept jumping back and forth between the men and the growing number of trout I saw bobbing to the surface of the lake. Needing to flee the scene of a supreme, yet unfinished adventure ran completely against James' nature. However, we'd never seen these men before, and decided to find a better hiding spot.

"Now that's what I call fishin'!" James yelled to no one in particular as we ran. When we were hid farther up the hill, we realized how badly our hearing had been hurt. His eyes, though, were popping out of his face and I saw that he could easily develop a strange hankering for dynamite fishing.

We watched as the men got down on their bellies and scooped in the trout close to the dock. As fish drifted within their reach, they nabbed them too. The smaller of the two men kept looking around. Obviously, he was wondering who set off the bomb that stunned these fish. But then he went back to work. This thievery got James seriously peeved.

"Those are our fish, darn it!" he snarled in a louder than normal whisper.

"Not anymore," I said, feeling sad as I read his lips.

The men worked at stealing our fish for a while and it was obvious we weren't going to get back down there, so we found our bikes and disappeared. James was so mad that those men spoiled the first fishing trip he'd actually enjoyed, he never wanted to do it again. Which was just fine with me. The blast started to wear off and we could talk to each other without sounding like two old codgers.

Looking at all those lunkers floating on the surface like bathtub toys really bugged me. Seeing them stolen bugged me more.

Anyway, because of the dynamite ordeal and the trout thieves, we'd taken the back trail home, and here we were, in the woods trying to figure out what to do with this dead guy.

* * *

Once the initial shock wore off, James hunkered down for a closer look. Most kids would have backed away from that much adventure. Not James Nelson. He was drawn to things that made others cringe. The stranger, the better.

I am not lying if I tell you that a week didn't go by where we were not in some kind a jam. But we always got out of it. Well, almost always.

And, generally speaking, neither of us was ever the scaredy-cat type. James never seemed to be scared. To be honest, I had my moments.

James approached life with the curiosity of a cat. He'd poke his nose down just about any hole. And if that didn't work, he'd shove his arm in. I just hoped he had all the lives that cats were supposed to have, cuz he was using them up faster than the average kid. He just didn't get rattled, but took life as it came along, in a relaxed manner.

During big Pop Warner football games, he didn't seem all that different than at practice. Big math and spelling tests he took in stride, even though he never did too well. It was his level head that also sucked me along with him. His easy-going attitude was hypnotic, which dragged me into situations where I wasn't relaxed.

He just had a way of making everything seem so natural, like it was meant to happen . . . and we were the guys for the job.

So when James moved closer to that body and lifted the branches covering the man's face with a stick, I did my level best to resist that sudden and familiar pull to come along for the ride. But when his expression hinted that what was under there was more than just the rest of the legs, I couldn't help it; my body slowly floated off that stump and I pretty much had a front row seat to what James was seeing.

James kind of squinted and pinched his lips together. I'd seen that look before on him when we found a dead dog under the bridge. It wasn't real fresh and James had made that same face.

"Pretty bad?"

He just nodded and moved the stick around.

"Who is it?" I whispered with growing interest.

"Dunno. You tell me. Boxcar bum probably." His answer held just a hint of disappointment.

Secretly, I think we both hoped it would be someone we knew; someone from town who'd stumbled out here drunk and dropped dead, and we could be in on solving the mystery. But, we hadn't heard of anyone not turning up, or the sheriff out and about searching for one of our less active citizens. Yep, it was probably a hobo.

Mud Lake, Washington was on a secondary line for the Union Pacific railroad, and every now and then boxcars deposited bums into our three alleys and one abandoned grange. There wasn't much to eat in a town that didn't have much and wasted even less, and the garbage from our only cafe and country store couldn't support even one bum for more than a month.

For that reason, the old derelicts soon crawled back into their boxcars and made for greener pastures, hopefully brimming with chicken bones and expired milk. So how this scruffy fellow ended up in the woods, five miles out of town, only added to the mystery. Gram said they were all God's kids, but James and I thought God must've forgotten a bunch of his kids when it came to hobos.

James was looking close.

"His head's been bashed pretty good, but I ain't no expert or coroner," he stated with authority. "They're kind a like people who open up dead people to see what killed 'em. They do autopsies 'n stuff."

"I know what a coroner is," I said weakly, sickened by the thought. "Who'd wanna paw around inside dead people?" It wasn't really a question so much as a statement of how my stomach suddenly felt.

"Coroners, that's who. It's how they figure out how folks died, stupid."

One of the few things James liked about school was science. He liked to use ten-dollar words to sound like an expert. He'd sometimes forget that because Gramps had done veterinary work on the side, I knew a few things myself.

"But, this guy . . . he's been bashed, that's what sucked the juice outta him," James spoke with a knowing sense of fact.

Again, he nudged the limp and rubbery corpse with

the stick.

"He ain't been dead too long, though," James observed.

"Wadda ya mean, James? Not too long."

"Rigor ain't set in."

"Oh, yeah, rigor mortis," I groaned, suddenly flashing back to when we'd found a dead muskrat last summer.

"It's the rigor mortis," James had said when we found the muskrat, looking up at me with a wild crazy look he always gets when an idea strikes him. "Hey, let's slice him open and do an autopsy."

At first I was not in favor of slicing open that bloated muskrat. But, like I told ya, James has this way of layin' things out to sound like the coolest thing since gas engines. He could have suggested cutting me open and pretty soon I might have gone along with it.

So, the thought of a coroner pawing around inside this old drunk was working on my stomach and the peanut butter sandwich I'd eaten earlier.

"Come look at this," James said with a sense of awe as he stooped to look closer. He was working his magic on me again, and pretty soon I was gawking over his shoulder. I instantly knew I'd made a bad decision.

Using the stick, James turned the man's face, exposing a bloody grimace and rearranged features. His misplaced teeth and broken nose made him look like one of those paintings by that French painter our art teacher liked so much. You know, the one with face parts all over the page . . . Pistachio, or something.

My stomach was finally mad at my eyes for looking and without warning my peanut butter sandwich kicked open the door of my tummy. Before I could turn away, that sandwich, my Nehi soda, and a Hershey bar came out like a volcano?. . . right on James' head and back. He instantly jumped up, knocking me to the ground.

"AH!" he yelled, while trying to shimmy out of his

thin coat.

"I'm sorry, James! That is the grossest thing . . ."

He didn't hear me. James furiously wiped chunks of vomit out of his hair and off his neck using the inside of his coat. Flinging the stained and stinking jacket to the ground, he glared at me.

"Ya barfed on me, man!"

"I'm sorry," I said with sincerity, in between spitting and convulsing. "The guy's teeth are falling out!"

"It's because he was murdered, stupid! Someone smashed him with somethin' . . . . I can't believe you barfed on me . . . you owe me for that."

We both knew that I'd be payin' him back all year.

He pulled out a handkerchief, wet it from his Scout canteen, and wiped his face and neck.

After one of his famous "I'm-gonna-kill-you-later" looks, he went back to examining our find.

As he again pulled the branches back, I was drawn by some strange attraction to look again into those half open eyes, with the kind of sleepy look. Whoever had worked him over had arranged his features into a disheveled smirk. The old hobo looked like he was laughing at me. His frozen expression hinted that he'd gotten the last laugh somehow, that making me barf was what he'd had in mind from the get-go. I swallowed hard, determined not to see lunch again.

"He's been beat bad," I whispered low.

I forced my eyes to look elsewhere and they landed on his well-traveled pants, with their collection of stains and dirt. One knee had been patched with a different material and the pockets were turned out, the result of his mugging I figured.

My instincts said, RUN! Tell someone there's a dead hobo in the woods!

"We gotta tell someone about this guy, right?" I asked. "Who should we tell? Gram'll know who to tell.

Or, your pa. He'd know."

James, however, didn't seem to share my concern. He just kept on poking and prodding the dead hobo with the stick, lifting his arm or his shirt.

"Maybe we shouldn't tell anyone . . . at least not right off."

And then he got that sly "this-is-a-great-idea" look.

"What if we did our own autopsy?" he said.

"What? Are you nuts? With what? My pocket knife?"

My stomach lurched a little at the thought of his genuine hair-brained idea . . . and me providing the tools.

"We can use yer Gramps' vet stuff," James said simply, warming to his idea.

"I think I'm gonna puke again."

I grabbed the canteen and took a swig to swish out the terrible taste in my mouth.

"Come on James, let's get the heck outta here."

James just sat back and looked at the hobo. He turned slowly to me.

"Wouldn't Mr. Phil have a baby if we walked into science class with a human heart?" He rolled his head around and looked at me with hysterical eyes. "Wait, we could tell him it's a cow heart, but our friends would know the truth."

He snorted out a laugh just thinking about what that would all look like. I couldn't get past the part about performing an autopsy.

I'd heard enough. I jumped up and instantly felt dizzy. I wobbled over to grab my bike, hoping it would encourage him to follow. I was determined to not let it go any further.

"I'm leaving. I'll wait for you at the road," I said as I hopped on and started off down the narrow path.

It was one of the rare times that I actually took the lead.

It wasn't that I was just a follower, it was that James was such a great leader. His ideas were nearly always full of adventure and busted us out of Mud Lake's boredom. And yeah, often it came around to a whipping from Uncle Neal or hard labor in Gram's giant garden. But, hanging around with James sure beat what most of the other kids were doing for fun. Except, doodlin' around with a mangled old body was just too much adventure for me.

* * *

I'd sat off to the side of the road for about fifteen minutes when James finally showed up. It was starting to get dark and I was just about to leave when he came peddling Pell Mell out of the gloomy woods with his hackles up and his eyes buggin' out of his face.

"Quick, ditch in the woods!" he hissed as he ripped past me and into the dense woods on the far side of the two-track road. I followed without thinking.

"What?" I whispered with fear and excitement.

It was pretty common for us to have to hiss and whisper, since our lives were frequently on the edge of danger. I just knew the murderers had come back to finish some evil deed and had seen James.

"He's followin' me!" James hissed back, with eyes the size of eggs.

"What? Who?" I asked. "The murderer?"

James looked at me like I was nuts.

"No, the body, you idiot!"

I'm sure, for a full three seconds, I stared at him. The hair on the back of my neck instantly jumped straight up, and I instinctively hunkered deeper into the shrubs. James got down next to me and watched too.

"I'm serious, Cal, now stay low. Dead guys have great night vision."

He then looked at me and, in the fading light, I instantly detected the corners of his mouth starting to curl up a bit. I gave him a shove that knocked him over and I jumped on him.

"You're full a . . . !"

He was laughing so hard that his mouth was a gaping hole, inviting revenge. I made him eat leaves, which he spit out and continued laughing.

James could have whipped me in a flash, but his laughter made him weak with humor and I took full advantage of the moment.

Satisfied, I jumped up, and acting mad, grabbed my bike and started off down the road.

"You should have seen your face when I tore past you," he shouted while getting his bike. "Man, you looked like the devil was after me!"

He'd got me good, that was for sure. And I was gonna get it even worse if the guys at school found out. I could hear him laughing behind me.

"Wait up," he yelled.

I didn't.

<h1 style="text-align:center">◇ CHAPTER 2 ◇</h1>

Buster's Squeamish Stomach

Buster Milts' eyes just about popped out of his face, and then he dropped to his knees. Twinkies and the entire school lunch menu exploded from his mouth with such force that even James was impressed.

When James poked the dead man's face and showed off his false teeth and mismanaged features, we got an added bonus as Buster keeled over with the dry heaves. James and me looked at each other and grinned.

We started calling our dead hobo Harold—outta respect, I guess, and so we could talk about him in terms other than "the dead bum" or "the stiff." Plus, the dead guy having a name made it seem like he was kind of our pal. The name just sort of forced its way on us.

"Harold?"

"Yeah, Harold!"

So, when James came up with the great idea of selling looks to our friends, Harold became part of our new money making scheme.

At first, the thought of going back into the woods and looking at Harold's bizarre face peeking out of the maples had little appeal for me. But, of course, James—the future car salesman or something—convinced me that we could make some serious money.

"Cal, it's cold at night. He'll keep," James explained when I protested that the geezer would start to stink, and no one's gonna want to see a stinky dead wino. Buster's instant barfing and willingness to hand over a week's worth of milk money proved me wrong.

* * *

"A dead guy? Where?" Buster blurted out when we told him about Harold. "Wait'll I tell Hermy!"

That had been my first concern. "How we gonna keep a lid on this? Guys are gonna blab."

"We make that part of the deal. We'll tell 'em we'll put 'Harold parts' in their locker if they blab and they'll get blamed for the murder," he instantly created, adding a grin for special effect. "Think about that for a minute!"

"What? Where're we . . . ? Oh no you don't." I saw where he was going. He was still thinking about some kind of autopsy.

"Relax, Cal. We won't need to do anything like that. Just the thought of a wino's finger found in their locker'll be enough to clamp 'em down tight."

But, when Buster's excitement risked a sudden outburst on the school playground, one that might involve his brother, Hermy, James devised an even better plan . . . at least for Buster.

"Oh, telling Hermy? That's not a good idea, Buster. You see, we're helpin' the cops with their investigatin' and they asked us to show the corpse to only you first."

James always spoke with such conviction that if I didn't know Harold and the truth, I might have believed him. He was a masterful storyteller, who never really meant to hurt anyone, just protect the interests of whatever project we were working on.

I always left the initial yarn to him. That way, I could gauge which way the wind was gonna blow. That's when I would generally jump in.

"Yeah, and we have to charge you something for the look, you see," my voice low and serious.

"Cuz they're bringing in some guys from Portland to work on the case and don't have the extra money to pay 'em," James added.

Buster nodded his head that this all made sense to him.

I could tell James was impressed by my story additions.

Now, I should probably mention that Buster was probably three bricks short of a load and would believe just about anything, which is why we'd decided to try out our plan on him first. We wanted to work on our story and get it fixed up before popping it on the smarter guys, like Marv or Stan.

James leaned in close to Buster and looked around slyly. "After school, you meet us behind the grange hall. And you better tell Hermy you're gonna go over to the store and help Mr. Burke bag tatters or somethin'."

"Remember, Buster, not a word or the cops'll have to step in," I added for emphasis.

* * *

We were pretty certain that Buster would keep his trap shut, because he was again lying on his side, cat-yackin' and spitting. The funny thing is, even lying there, he couldn't take his eyes off Harold. I offered Buster my canteen of water.

"Thanks," he moaned weakly.

He slurped a big wet swig and swished it around and spit it out of his mouth. I knew that was the last time I'd ever use that canteen.

"That's reeeally gross, guys," Buster said. "That guy's really dead?"

James just rolled his eyes and I chimed in.

"He's been here for days. Yeah, he's dead."

"Hey, Buster, wanna see his eyes?" James said slyly.

"His eyes?"

Buster rubbed his own eyes, wanting to cover them, but also, not.

"Yeah, you paid the money," James said, "You should get the full deal."

He slowly pulled up the branches to again reveal the old wino's face. Even though the fall weather was chilly, the man had taken on a waxy yellowish appearance. The effect was even more shocking than when we'd nearly tripped on the guy last Saturday.

"Lookie there, Milts," James said low and motioned for Buster to come closer to the contorted corpse. James' sly encouragement acted like a magnet, and Buster slid closer and peered into the maples.

"See, his eyes ain't closed," James whispered. "Kind a spooky don't ya think? It's like he's lookin' right at ya."

It looked like they were. Those milky, half open eyes were looking right at Buster Milts. I was certain he'd have nightmares for years to come.

* * *

I know . . . I'd already had a couple of nightmares, myself.

I woke up last night after a dream where Harold was sitting at the kitchen table having morning coffee with Gramps, who also didn't look altogether healthy, having been dead for a year now.

Well, while I sat there eating my cereal, listening to them talk about being dead and all, every now and then Harold would look at me with those milky eyes. When he smiled, a tooth'd fall out into his coffee and make a little splash. Then Gramps'd say "oops" and give that little chuckle he always gave when something tickled him good.

Harold would fish his tooth out with a spoon and pop it back in his mouth.

Then Gramps said, "Be sure ya get it in the right spot there."

Gramps smiled at me and winked. I woke up right after the wink . . . and checked my own teeth, top and bottom.

* * *

For that reason, I mostly watched James' expression of enjoyment rather than add to my own overtaxed memories of Harold's freakish features. He may have been one of our pals, but I didn't appreciate him messing around in my dreams.

Buster simply stared at the unearthly face peering back at him from the golden maple leaves. Milts' own expression slowly started to mimic the hobo in the bushes. He turned his head to the side and his lips kind of curled up, revealing his own misplaced teeth.

I gave James a little head nod and he grinned. He was loving every minute of scaring the crud out of Buster Milts.

We should have charged more for this, I thought. I need to bring that up when we get home.

"Wadda ya thinka that, Milts?" James asked, gauging Buster's shock.

"It's reeeeal gross, guys," he simply stated again.

"Any idea what killed him?" I asked, trying to bring the police investigation back into the conversation. James pocked at the man's ashen face to make it move and reveal more of his deadly injuries. I stole a glance and noticed maggots using Harold's nose as a door to his brain. I instantly looked away, feeling suddenly swoony.

"Oh, gaw . . . ," I muttered, and looked over at James, who I could tell by his twisted smile and crazy eyes found this new addition fascinating.

"Looks like someone bashed him with a bat," Buster slowly concluded.

"You mean, like a baseball bat?" James asked.

"Yeah. Like a Louisville. Like mine." Buster's words were slow and thoughtful, his face still contorted. He was really trying to figure out what had happened to this poor unlucky hobo.

At that moment I heard voices way off in the woods.

"Shush," I hissed. "Listen!"

We stopped and listened carefully. They were older voices, and they were coming our way.

"Come on!" James ordered. We all grabbed our bikes and dashed down the tiny trail that was the back way to Mud Lake.

James veered off the trail about fifty yards from Harold's hiding place, and me and Buster followed. We tucked into some thick maples and peered out.

"What are we doing this for?" I asked in a muted voice. "Let's get the heck outta here!"

"I wanna see who it is," James replied.

"I don't," Buster said.

"What if it's someone with a bat?" I asked in a low voice. I hadn't realized I'd said it out loud until James and Buster both looked at me. I looked back and nodded. "What if . . . ?"

"Well, it's too late now," James whispered, pointing.

Two tough looking characters emerged from the forest—the same two men we'd seen collecting our stunned trout. James and me looked at each other.

"That's the guys at the lake," he whispered. I nodded.

Close up, we could see that these were men who'd lived on the outer edges of decency. Their clothes were faded and stained and thin at the knees. Their unshaved faces and greasy long hair just added more nastiness to their already grubby appearance. But it was the coldness in their eyes that stood out to me. The fact that we were close enough to see their eyes also had me terrified.

The bigger one had hands like catcher's mitts. The other one, the skinny fellow, moved with a twitchy, nervous awareness of his surroundings. It was like he expected someone to jump out and club him.

I could see in James' expression that he'd like to jump up and take them on. I have to admit, something in me was suddenly agitated and hungered for revenge because of the trout incident. I knew it was a terrible idea, though, and slowly grabbed a handful of James' shirt, just in case.

Like I said, having them thirty yards away from us, I could easily see that these were not nice guys, and because of what happened next, I wished we'd not hung around.

The big guy gave the little guy a shove. It wasn't a "fun" shove either; he almost knocked him down.

"So, where is he?" the big one demanded. He grabbed the skinny one with one of his huge mitts and gave him another shove.

"Somewhere around here," the skinny one snarled back. "It was damn dark that night."

He started tossing branches and then he found the blindfold we'd used on Buster to conceal Harold's exact location.

"What's this?" he asked, holding up the scarf.

"Uh oh," I moaned.

"Someone's been here," the big man said, and instantly cast nervous glances around the woods. We right away made ourselves smaller behind the bushes.

Well, crud, I thought to myself. We may as well have stood up and said, "We're over here, boys."

"And they puked," the smaller man noticed and pointed to the ground.

Then they found Harold.

Buster started to sniffle and I put my arm around him.

"Buster, this is a real bad time to become a cry baby," I whispered, my mouth closer than I'd ever imagined being to another kid's ear. "Put a cork in it."

The men grabbed Harold's legs and roughly dragged him out into the open.

"Whew, Ike," said the larger man, looking at Harold's face. "Ya pulverized 'im!"

Ike just shrugged and looked kind of sheepish, like he was sorry or something.

"Well, Dreggs, you sure you don't wanna just bury him right here?"

"If'n you'd done what I told ya, we wouldn't be standin' 'er smellin' old Jenkins," Dreggs said in a tone that was angry and real put out.

James and me exchanged a look. I could see in his eyes "that look." Now, I started to get worried about what James might do.

"It was dark I told ya, and he wasn't too keen on me killin' him, neither," the man named Ike complained.

"You're always full'a excuses," Dreggs said while looking at Jenkins' lifeless body. He again glanced around the forest. "Come on, let's get this done with. I got a bad feelin'."

He shoved Ike, who made a punch back, but missed, and they grabbed Jenkins.

"We're gonna just take 'im all the way back to camp?" Ike asked.

None of us could hear Dreggs' response. But he didn't look too happy. They half carried, half dragged Jenkins—and his maggots—off into the forest, back the way they had come.

"Let's go," I urged.

Buster was trying to hold back tears and nodding his head that he also wanted to leave.

"Wait," James cautioned. "Let them get up the trail before we come out. What if they're just hiding and waiting for us to pop out?"

"They're not doin' that," I said. "They're haulin' that Jenkins fellow off somewhere. Come on."

Hiding out for a few minutes to see who that red bandana belonged to would be something James would do. He didn't understand that few people thought like him.

James watched and thought, shushing my next objection.

"You take Buster back to town," he said. "I'm gonna see if I can find out where their camp is."

"Are you nuts?" I whispered, maybe a little too loud. "Those guys killed Harold . . . Jenkins . . . whoever he is . . . was."

"That's why I'm gonna find out where they're holed up," James argued.

"Let's just slip outta here and let the sheriff know what we saw," I countered.

"Yeah, let the sheriff," Buster started to agree, but James cut him off.

"Oh, Sheriff Stubbs. That's a great idea," James hissed, annoyed with our chicken attitude. "By the time he gets here from Salmon those guys'll be all the way to Stevensville." He glared at me and Buster, letting the truth sink in.

He was right. Sheriff Stubbs was thirty miles away and almost always arrived too late. There was a general attitude among Mud Lake's hundred and fifty residents that calling the sheriff in a crisis was a general waste of time.

Most everyone dealt with hard situations themselves, and figured Providence would do the rest. The joke was that even God couldn't depend on old Sheriff Stubbs.

James knew he was right, and suddenly dashed off into the woods, planning to circle around and catch the men up the trail a bit.

We both knew these woods like our own bedrooms, and even though I was scared, I also knew that James could stay hid while discovering something of value.

"Come on," I said and shoved Buster toward our bikes.

When Buster and I hit the two-track road, I stopped; figuring I'd better put a spit shine on our secret and tighten the button on Buster's lips. As it turned out, I didn't need to do much polishing or buttoning . . . the huge wet spot on his pants gave away that Buster was twice as scared as me.

"Did you pee your pants, Buster?" I asked with one part disgust and one part laughter. "What's Hermy gonna say about that if I tell him?"

"Come on, Cal," Buster whined. "Don't tell Hermy."

"Only if you keep your mouth shut about all this," I ordered while thumping my index finger on his chest.

I went on to add that if he yapped to anyone about Harold and what we'd seen he might never see his Ma and Hermy again cuz the police might suspect it was him that killed that bum. Never mind that we'd just seen the guys who did it. The thing about Buster is when he was scared he forgot everything else.

"You do have a Louisville Slugger, Buster," I reminded him. "And cuz it's not in your room, but hid in your garage, they'd suspect something." I didn't actually know where his bat was kept, but I knew the suggestion that I did know would help.

"And, if they found any loose change in your pockets, they'd think it was that hobo's and that's what you and the old guy'd tussled over." I was on a roll and decided to pile it on deep. Buster was a known blabber mouth and we'd learned that we had to practically threaten his life to keep him quiet. I felt pretty good about him peein' in his pants, though.

My face contorted as I got a new thought. I decided to make Buster never ever even THINK about talking to anyone in the universe.

"What if one of those rascals has an inside track with the sheriff, and that big one found out it was you who seen them messin' around with the body?"

Buster's eyes got real big when I led him down that wild road.

"Yeah," I added for extra drama, "he looked like a guy who could put the hurt on someone real bad."

I could tell I'd gone far enough when Buster's eyes started welling up with tears.

"I ain't gonna tell no one, Cal. I don't wanna go to jail. My daddy was in jail and he told me it was no place for a kid, and that I should watch my ways or I'd end up there spendin' the night with winos."

He was crying now, so I decided I'd better stop after I gave him one last look, my best you-better-watch-out head nod and started off toward town. He fell in right behind and looked backwards almost all the way back to town, while I worried about James the rest of the way.

I felt kind of bad about telling Buster he might not see Hermy again, cuz they were so close. We all liked Hermy. He'd somehow gotten Buster's missing bricks and was pretty smart, helping us with our math sometimes when we got stumped. But Hermy was kind of a straight-laced type of kid and there was no tellin' what he'd do if he knew we'd shown his dumb little brother a dead wino, and charged him his milk money for the peek.

I learned years later that Buster had trouble sleeping after seeing old spooky Harold. His dreams were filled with dead, maggoty bodies. Harold scrambled around in my nightmares, too . . . along with what came next.

◇ **CHAPTER 3** ◇

Quiet Night in Mud Lake

It was almost completely dark by the time I stashed my bike in the breezeway between the shop and garage. I tried to slip quietly in the back door.

Even though it was Saturday night, I wasn't usually allowed out past dark, which is why I knew I'd have some explaining to do. Working on Buster to keep him quiet and worrying about James had taken most of my thinking time and I hadn't worked up a story, which suddenly struck me as dangerous.

I saw right off that Gram had already cleaned up dinner, and she and Uncle Neal were in the living room watching I Love Lucy.

There was a ritual at Gram's house—eat dinner on time and then monkey with the TV antenna all evening, searching in vain for a good picture. Most of the time it was my job to be the "antenna monkey," which is why I had my own pillow right in front on the floor. That way,

I was handy for quick orders from Gram or Uncle Neal.

At the moment I drifted in the door, Uncle Neal was up from his stuffed chair, tinkling with the rabbit ears. As usual, he was trying to get the steel bunny ears to better grab Lucy and Ethel while Gram coached from her chair.

"Neal, no . . . move 'em to the left a little," Gram whined. "Are they pulled out all the way? Sometimes I have to put them in for General Hospital."

"They're out all the way, Millie," Uncle Neal stated with his usual annoyance. "It's the weather tonight."

I'd seen some big dark boilers piled up over the mountains, so I knew Uncle Neal was right.

Many years later, someone would put a TV repeater up on one of the mountains, so Mud Lake could have "real" reception. It didn't matter that it was really crummy reception; everyone talked about it like it the next best thing to indoor plumbing. As far as Mud Lakers were concerned, it would be years before we were in the modern world.

Well, my internal rabbit ears were up too, checking to see what kind of trouble I was in for breezing in after dark. I could tell right off that Uncle Neal was grumpy, probably partly because he was up doing my job as TV reception supervisor. I knew I was in for a high level interrogation.

"Oh for cryin' out loud, Neal. Where's Cal?"

Gram suddenly noticed me standing in the doorway and stopped. Neal turned too.

"What's your story, young fella?" he said, with his hands frozen over the TV, looking kind of goofy.

I suddenly realized that's probably what I looked like when messing with the antenna, and I didn't like what I saw. He looked like the Scare Crow in the Wizard of Oz.

"We waited until all of our dinners got a cold," he added with a not too happy tone. "We waited and then we just went on and had dinner, didn't we, Millie."

Gram didn't want to bother with scolding me right then; she wanted to get back to Lucy and Ethel.

"There's chops and taters in the fridge, Hon," she said sweetly.

"I'm not so sure he should have dinner tonight, Millie. Strolling in here after dark like it's five o'clock."

"Neal, the picture," Gram blurted.

Uncle Neal just stood there, leaving the TV picture covered with snow.

"Just a second, Millie," he replied, not taking his eyes off me. "I dunno how many times I gotta tell you, Calvin—food's meant to be ate hot and yer supposed to be home on time."

In my head, I quoted the words in perfect step with Uncle Neal. You see, for Uncle Neal, a chilly meal would have ruined Jesus' last supper . . . even more than Calvary. It was as if he sat with his fork cocked and ready to stab whatever food hit the table. Sometimes he'd even burn his lips he liked his food so piping hot.

"Food's meant to be ate hot," was his constant needling when it came to being on time for meals.

"So, what was so important to almost ruin your Gram's good cookin'?"

"Ummmm . . ." I opened my mouth to speak and suddenly my brain locked up.

I figured it would be all over town the next day that someone had blasted a mess of fish up at Mosquito Lake, so I decided not to mention where James and I had been. I maintained my best stupid innocent smile and decided that Mill Pond would be my story.

"Well, James and me kind of lost track of time?. . . up at the Pond," I drawled out and trailed off like that was all there was to tell.

"That's why I'm late," I added.

It was a ways up to Mill Pond and in the opposite

direction, which could account for a late arrival.

"Eh, ah, the sun going behind Lookout Peak didn't give you a clue?" he questioned with contempt, looking back at the TV and moving the rabbit ears around.

"Well, yeah, but James was actually having fun. . ."

That was a big stretch, but Uncle Neal didn't really know that James hated fishing, unless explosives were involved.

He looked back at me with a suspicious expression. He was trying to detect the tattered threads of yarn in my story. My face worked into a kind of fuddled, wide-eyed mixture of smile and confusion. But suddenly, Harold the dead hobo and his bizarre sneer popped into my mind and I lost my concentration. I could feel my eyes glaze over and I was thrown back to staring at the old dead geezer with barf smell in my nose.

I could feel myself losing my momentum when Gram let out a burst of laughter. Uncle Neal and me both glanced at the TV. Lucy and Ethel were dressed in cooking clothes, with floppy white hats, sticking candies in their mouth as fast as they could.

"Neal, fix that picture!" Gram ordered. She was not generally the bossy type; like I said she was always nice and sweet, but the Lucy Show or Ed Sullivan covered in snow could raise up her hackles real quick.

Uncle Neal was forced to put off my scolding until we got Gram satisfied. He let me take over messing with the thin steel rods that somehow snagged our favorite shows out of the air and magically stuffed them into Gram's massive TV cabinet.

It was a bizarre ceremony—this messing with the TV—that, for years, drove much of rural America nuts.

"Neal, go get Cal his chops and tatters," she ordered, without taking her eyes off the TV. "Oh! Oh, there! Cal, don't move a muscle." She burst out laughing with her hand up in the air in a frozen position, trying to will the snow from the picture. Uncle Neal gave me a snarly look as he headed for the kitchen.

* * *

Even with crabby Uncle Neal orbiting around my life at Mud Lake, it was a ton better than Portland.

Things started to go goofy a few years back. Dad blamed Mom and Mom blamed Dad, which ended with a lotta yelling and slammed doors, and sometimes no dinner. I figure I spent about a year in my bedroom just keeping my head down. I soon learned that all that fighting was pretty normal for folks who didn't love each other anymore. So, when they decided to chuck it in, I was kind of glad cuz they stopped twisting each other's noses, and me and my sister could quit hidin' out in our rooms. I tried to explain it to my little sister, but she didn't understand all the big words. She also didn't understand why she had to go live with Mom and I went off to live with Dad. She cried a lot after I told her what was about to happen.

That's when I was around seven and Dad had that sales job that kept him on the road a lot. He hated being away and leaving me with the neighbor lady, Mrs. Harvey. I hated it too. She did some pretty nutty stuff, like rearranging the kitchen cabinets all the time and making me count the cream corn cans. The number was always bigger, which made her mad, because she didn't like cream corn. The problem I figured out was that cream corn was always on sale and she couldn't pass it up. She also cooked those Swanson Chicken Pot Pies almost every night and I finally puked on them. To this day, just seeing them in the freezer case at the store makes my throat squeeze shut.

Anyway, when Dad found out that she had some kind of sickness that makes people forget things—dismantled or dismented or something is what he called it—he worked it out for me to come live with Gram and Gramps.

Coming to live at Mud Lake was great. Of course, I put on a sad face when Dad told me what was happening. I didn't want him to feel bad, like I didn't love him or nothing.

I'd always come up and stay with Gram and Gramps in the summer for a few weeks, but to live here, man, it was like stepping up to the pie table at the fair and told to eat all I wanted. Well, until Uncle Neal showed up, that is. He was always trying to grab the fork out of my hand.

Uncle Neal was Gramps' younger brother who'd come to live with them a couple of months before Gramps had died. He said he came to help with chores and the animals, but I think it was to wrangle me. He pretty much took it upon himself to administer my discipline, which he said was lacking because Gram and Gramps were just about the nicest people ever born. He was of the outspoken opinion that I was just too wild for his older kin to deal with.

"I'll be darned if you're gonna run the roost around here, Calvin Poag," he assured me one day behind the barn, after I'd run Gramps' lawn tractor into the irrigation ditch. "You're a wild seed and you ain't gonna take root in your Gram's garden. Not if I have anything to say about it."

His face was so close I could smell his cigarette breath. I wasn't really all that wild, at least not by my standards. When laid up beside James, I wasn't even a sprout. Wait'll ya meet James, I thought, when he tried to shove me into the "wild" category.

James' pa was a truck driver and gone all the time, which left James to pretty much figure out life for himself. His ma was kind of nutty and didn't seem to even notice if James was around or not. Of course, having six younger kids to deal with didn't help much either. Watching her try to corral all those kids was like watching someone try and swat flies in a milk parlor.

James could disappear for days and not really be missed all that much. But, for me, after Uncle Neal came on the scene, I was on a pretty short chain. If it wasn't for Gram and her sweetness, I wouldn't have had any fun.

Having spent so much time wiggling out of trouble with James taught me how to set my mouth and the tone of my voice just right to help sell whatever story I was selling. But when Uncle Neal arrived, it was as if he'd invented the technique and knew all the old tricks.

The fact is—and Gramps is the one who said it—Uncle Neal got more than his share of orneriness. And something about me just made him ooze "ornery."

* * *

It was kind of cold on Gram's back porch after dark, but I sat out there anyway and nibbled my pork chop and listened to Lucy and Ethel in the background. The bugs were gone for the summer and I was alone to try and sort out my thoughts. I would have liked to watch TV, but figured it might be safer out here. The whole thing with dead Harold and his nasty friends coming along and dragging him off really popped me out of gear, and I felt that I needed to not be around folks who could read me pretty well.

It was hard though—I loved Lucy too. She and Ethel reminded me a little of James and me. Only they always managed to wiggle out of their troubles by the end of the show; our "wigglin'" sometimes went on for days.

We actually tried to figure out what it was they did to swing things their way and looked at I Love Lucy as a kind of getting out of trouble manual. Of course, we both knew it wasn't real, but we also figured the person writing the show must have been kind of like us as a kid and so we watched carefully for patterns of escape

In fact, and you better not say nothin' about this, the face I'd just tried on Uncle Neal when telling him I was up at the Mill Pond was a face I'd seen Lucy use on Ricky a lot of times. Her mouth would get kind of screwed over to one side with her eyes wide open. That was the face I was using on Uncle Neal right then.

I wasn't very hungry and just picked at my pork chop and potatoes. Images of Harold's grin kept elbowing their way into my mind. I also couldn't stop wondering what had happened with James. The road out of town ran right past Gram's and I kept craning my neck, hoping to see him come bombing up to let me know what he'd found. I knew it would be something crazy.

I was nibbling on my pork chop when Leopold, Gram's dog, came around the corner and parked at the top of the steps. Leo could sniff out food a mile off and was my constant companion when I was eating on the porch.

"Hey boy, glad you weren't with us today," I whispered to Leo, who sat patiently waiting for his scraps. "You'd of barked at those gangsters for sure." He just wagged his tail, eyeing my plate.

Gram made the best chops, and I could usually put away two or three of her fried specialty. But tonight, Leo got almost a full pork chop and the rest of my mashed potatoes. He wolfed down his treats and was expertly crunching on the bone when Uncle Neal came out.

"Oh, you're out here. How come you're not watchin' Lucy?" he said with a hint of suspicion.

I licked my fingers as a show of how fast I must have eaten and swallowed an imaginary mouthful.

"Ah, well, I've seen that one." It was a pretty lame excuse because the candy factory episode was one of my favorites.

He lit a Camel and blew out a big puff of smoke, eyeing me carefully.

"Eh," he scoffed, and sucked on his cigarette. "So, how was the fishin'?"

"We didn't catch nothin'," I replied with a note of disappointment.

Uncle Neal turned to me on that one. He knew I was a good fisherman and me not catching anything wasn't normal. I knew I better spice up my story, and fast.

"Nothing worth keeping, I mean."

He sucked on his cigarette and just looked at me.

"Yeah, ya really need a boat to get out where the big ones are," he added, like he knew what he was talking about.

Uncle Neal didn't really like fishing all that much, but he'd heard Gramps say that once and repeated it like it was his own idea. I knew better, but didn't say anything.

Lucky for me, right then the dog coughed a huge yack and started to choke. Neal looked at Leopold for a moment, assessing his situation.

"Did you give him that chop bone?" he asked accusingly.

"I just . . ."

"Come here!" He grabbed Leo and started digging in his mouth. Leo fought him and tried to chew Neal's fingers.

"Ow, dern you, Leo," Neal snapped and glanced back at me. "Well, it's not your fault, ya dumb dog."

He pried the bone out and massaged Leo's throat until another chunk popped out. Neal stood up and showed the bones to me.

"See how sharp that is? You want that stuck in your throat?" He glared at me and went inside.

I was saved twice in the same evening—once by Lucy and our horrible television reception and then by Leo and the pork bone. I felt like Superman dodging bullets. In the world of kid economics, that added up to a good day's profits.

I suddenly noticed that Uncle Neal had forgotten his Camel. It sat there on the concrete rail, about half smoked. I watched the thin line of smoke slither upwards in the still night air.

Besides some pretty good whippin's for me, Camel's are one of the other things Uncle Neal brought to Gram's and Gramps' house. I'd watched Uncle Neal sit and smoke out here while he and Gramps discussed the day's events. He made smoking look like an important part of life's scheme. He kind of made it look cool, which is why I snitched a couple right after he came. But that's when I learned that people were just acting cool when they puffed those things, because if you ask me, the taste was pretty nasty. I never picked up another one.

A lot of kids I knew snitched smokes from their folks. A couple of guys could blow smoke rings, and Hank Greggs could blow smoke out his nose, which was pretty funny. I guess smoking was okay, if you wanted to look cool. But James and me preferred to be cool, not just act cool. Most of the guys we knew who tried to look cool with cigarettes weren't guys I'd hang out with.

We took one particularly heavy smoker kid on an outing one time and the kid wouldn't even go into a mineshaft. He just stood there sniveling and whining that we'd all get hurt. That's when we decided that smoking wasn't all that cool. Anyone could smoke and try to look cool, but having your very own dead body stashed in the woods. Now that was cool!

We'd found the body and messed around with it, but no one had to know that part . . . or that I had barfed.

I felt pretty sure James wouldn't tell anyone about that. And we'd charged Buster money to look at it. That was all cool stuff.

As I started thinking about what James and me had been up to, I started feeling kind of smug. And knowing it was stupid, something inside me suddenly wanted to steal a puff off Uncle Neal's Camel.

I was partly in motion when the screen door opened and Uncle Neal reappeared.

I swung down in a fluid arch and started petting Leo, who'd come over for reassurance after his bone robbery. Uncle Neal just grabbed his cigarette, took a long drag, snuffed it out and tossed it over the side into Gram's chrysanthemums.

"Don't give that dog no more bones, Cal," he snapped at me and went back inside.

Having dodged trouble on two occasions, I recognized that my luck coupons were spent for that day and decided to go to bed.

But as it turned out, I didn't get much sleep.

◇ CHAPTER 4 ◇

Strange Splash Off Granite Point

The first time my dad had to wake me up at four thirty in the morning to go pick raspberries was the last time. Dad wasn't much of a morning person, and the fact that the sun wouldn't be up for another two hours made his methods all the more unpleasant.

Dad was big on using what I called the Big Light— the overhead light in my room.

"That's how they woke us in the army, and by gosh, if it's good enough for me, it's good enough for you," he barked when I complained bitterly. I know he'd fixed it with a hundred watt bulb for added effect.

That very day though, the day I started my career as a fruit harvester, he ran me down right after work to Meier & Frank's department store and bought me an alarm clock. He'd even sprung for one with a lighted face, which is what I'd wanted. My plan was to get it myself after I got paid for picking. But Dad spared me the expense. I didn't bother to tell him I'd been planning it anyway, wanting to avoid the pain of repayment.

I loved the lighted face. Sometimes, I'd lie there and watch the second hand make its trip around the numbers before falling to sleep.

The lighted face was how I knew that it was three in the morning when James woke me up, tapping on my window. I rolled over and saw him peering in, looking very nervous, or excited. It was sometimes hard to tell the difference. He was saying something, but since the weather had started turning chilly at night, Uncle Neal made me shut my window.

"It kicks on the furnace, Calvin, when you leave yer window open," Neal complained.

I liked the cool air washing over my head at night. It reminded me of sleeping out in the woods.

I had to be very careful opening the window. It made a loud scratch if it wasn't raised just right. James tried to help from the outside, but I scolded him.

"I gotta do it from in here or it'll squeak," I whispered. "Where the heck you been, anyway?"

"I'll tell ya. Come on," he whispered back.

I scrambled into my clothes, being careful to miss all the floor squeaks. I had them all memorized. The floor of my upstairs room was like a minefield of squeaks, so that any "past bedtime activities" had to be done with military precision.

I gently shut the window so the furnace wouldn't kick on, being careful to leave a crack for getting back in, and we climbed down the apple tree that grew near the garage.

Once away from the house, we flopped down behind the barn.

"They've got their little camp set up about a mile from Granite Point," James summarized. He wasn't one to go on and on when a quick recap would do.

"What'd they do with Harold, I mean Jenkins?" I asked quietly.

"They just dumped him in the lake?off Granite Point," he stated with a mixed tone of annoyance and indifference. I could tell he was pretty put out that Dreggs and Ike had nabbed our new pal, and we'd lost out on at least a week's worth of fun scaring the puke out of our friends. I could also tell he was onto something new, something even bigger.

"They put rocks in his pants pockets and just rolled him over into the water. He sank fast," James explained. I could tell he was just a tiny bit impressed with the rocks in the pockets part. I think he thought it might be something he would've done . . . if he were evil.

The water off Granite Point was estimated to be forty or fifty feet deep. It was probably the deepest part of the lake, and, of course, our favorite swimming hole. The low cliffs that shot straight down into the blue depths afforded dramatic diving. My brain started working and I looked hard at James.

"So," I said, "Jenkins' clean-picked bones and his surly grin will be staring up at our wrinkled feet."

James got suddenly serious as he considered that thought.

"Darn strangers scummin' up our waterhole," he said.

That did it for me. No more swimming at Granite Point. I'd just have to say that I'd developed a keen dislike for water that cold. I didn't have any idea what James would say. He'd probably borrow someone's diving gear and go down there to look at him. The thought made a shiver run up my spine.

"Just dumped him off the point," I muttered.

"Yeah."

Just then, Chaps—Gramps' ancient mare—made that sound happy horses make. I think the old guys called it nickering. She knew it was me and wanted a treat, which I generally had when I went out to see her.

"Come on." James jumped up and started off across Gram's pasture. I had no choice but to follow. If I shouted at him to stop, I'd awaken all the animals, not to mention Uncle Neal and his 20-gauge. We'd had a varmint problem this year and Uncle Neal had taken to keeping his shotgun handy. So, we kept our voices low. Uncle Neal's hearing far outran his lousy eyesight.

I caught up with James at the irrigation ditch under the Cotton Woods. "Where are we going?"

"Back. We gotta get more information," James stated like this was the most natural thing to do at three in the morning.

"I can't leave," I stammered.

"Why not? We got a couple hours before anyone gets up. We can get up there, check things out, and be back in two hours."

Here I was again, faced with what I knew was a stretch and James' view of logic. He was right; we could make the round trip in two hours, and probably collect enough evidence to help the sheriff catch these thugs. But, then my mind suddenly stuck on sheriff Stubbs.

"And do what with that information?"

I knew that James was probably wingin' it right there on the spot . . . and probably hadn't added Sheriff Stubbs into his plans. On the other hand, it had been drilled into me that Stubbs—Uncle Neal preferred to drop the sheriff title—lacked any professional abilities.

I really had no other way of knowing if Stubbs was as bad as everyone said . . . no one tells kids anything. But the fact that most folks around Mud Lake dropped the sheriff part when they talked about him, and the stream of ribbing Stubbs attracted—both to his face and behind his back—told me people didn't think very highly of him.

So, here I was, about to risk a royal whipping from

Uncle Neal about information that I was uncertain would end up in competent hands. James gave me a little shove. He could tell I wasn't game yet.

"Hey, even if Stubbs doesn't show up in time, we'll still be the coolest cats in town."

I guess he had factored in Stubbs' reputation after all.

"We don't know what those two guys'd do to us if they caught us," I stated boldly. The picture of the two of us with rearranged faces and misplaced teeth suddenly popped into my head.

"There's a great place for us to hide out and just watch 'n see what they're up to," said James. "And when I was watchin' 'em, it looked like they might be hittin' the trail soon. Come on . . . ."

James jumped up and scrambled through the trees to his bike, and you know what, that rascal had my bike stashed there too!

There's something inside kids like us that makes us not want to miss out on stuff no one else knows about. Add to that James' natural excitement and I was soon pumping my bike peddles in high gear with the cool night air chilling my peach fuzz head.

We rounded the corner on the edge of town, near the old grange hall, and there was a train blocking the road.

This was the train I told you about that pulls into town once a month and deposits goods and the occasional vagrant.

"Any idea what time it is?" James asked without looking at me.

"It was ten after three when we climbed out the window," I remembered. "So . . . probably three thirty."

"I thought it's supposed to leave at three," James said.

At that moment, the loud metallic scratch and clang

of car hitches started working its way down the train. We'd both heard it a hundred times; the sound each car makes when its hitch jams against the next. The succession of bangs was getting closer and faster, and we had to decide; wait for the train to move, which could take ten or fifteen minutes, or make a dash through the cars and risk getting squashed between boxcars.

We'd jumped cars before . . . most of the kids we knew did. So, we knew what to expect. But at night, with our bikes, and scared to boot, this was a little different.

James jumped off his bike and started to run between the boxcars. The fact that James didn't hesitate more than a second didn't surprise me; the fact that I followed, and made it, did. We both stood for a second, close to the cars we'd just cleared, and watched them jerk violently, and then start to move.

We'd once again cheated death, or at least injury, to continue on our adventure chasing thieves and murderers.

I was suddenly filled with that sense of excitement, which I knew was a natural part of James' life. For the moment, it was grand, and we looked at each other wide-eyed. I knew from experience that that kind of heat pumping through my veins was more than I could handle every day.

"Come on," James whispered, "let's do it!"

"Wait . . . look . . ."

I'd noticed something down about twenty cars or so. Two men were tossing their bedrolls and another sack into a boxcar. The train was moving?. . . in our direction.

"That's them, Cal. The two who sank Harold. They're gettin' away. It's do it or die time, Cal!"

We ducked behind a loading dock and watched as they started trotting alongside the train. Dreggs jumped and scrambled aboard. Ike, the one with shorter legs, had to hustle faster to keep up with the train's growing speed. It wasn't that fast, but it took him until the car was about level with us for him to clamor aboard

Suddenly, James did the most unexpected thing. He darted out from our hiding spot and grabbed hold of the following car and dragged himself aboard. I watched, dumbfounded. Then he motioned for me to come too. My body reacted before my brain and I dropped my bike and dashed for the train car.

I think I've said it enough . . . I'm nowhere near as athletic as James, and now I was trotting along next to a moving locomotive and reaching for James' hand. I could feel the train speeding up as I was running out of gas. Then our hands grabbed each other and I almost lost my balance because James almost yanked me off my feet.

Now what? James was pulling me forward and I needed to get a foot on the rung and jump aboard. I couldn't shout out, for the obvious reason that Dreggs and Ike were up in the next car.

Finally, James gave me a big pull and somehow I found the foot rung and scrapped aboard.

Just as I crawled inside and was about the say something, I looked back at our two bikes, thinking I'd never see them again, and wondered what the police would say to my family about me being "kidnapped" by hobos. I suddenly noticed Dreggs poke his head out of their car and look forward. I scrambled out of sight and held my tongue.

I peeked out and didn't see Dreggs anymore, so I assumed he hadn't seen me. I wasn't sure though.

◇ CHAPTER 5 ◇

Bum in the Boxcar

James stood swaying, balancing against the movement of the train while I gathered my legs under me and crawled to my feet. Like I said before, we'd jumped a few trains, so we were used to the steady wobble they produced. It was hard to see in the gloom, so we both hung onto the weathered wood and squinted into the darkness of the creaky boxcar.

It wasn't full, but it wasn't empty either. There were fruit boxes and barrels scattered about and some stacked against the walls. The darkness made me feel very uncomfortable and I hung close to the door where I could see the hint of forest starting to pass at an ever-increasing speed.

It suddenly irked me that James was chuckling as he caught his breath. We hadn't run that far, so I knew it was probably excitement that was stealing his wind.

"What was that all about, anyway?" I asked in an

angry tone.

"I dunno, I just did it," he answered with a smile.

At moments like this James seemed to stand outside himself and be amazed at his scorn for danger. His amusement could be infectious, once the initial shock of finding ourselves alive and generally not too banged up. I was usually a late bloomer when it came to letting terror turn to relief. Once my legs stopped shaking, I might find the joy in the moment's spontaneous peril. Then the giggles. Not as often as James, though.

So, as I caught glimpses of James' sparkling eyes in the diminishing light, I could tell he was gauging my reaction to this new wrinkle at three thirty in the morning.

"Well, now what's the plan, smart guy?" I asked with a note of concern. "This won't be a two hour round trip now."

He snickered at my comment. He wasn't the one who'd get grounded for a week; it might take that long for his mom to even notice he was gone.

As I was eyeing him and thinking about giving him the satisfaction of a small smile, I noticed a scruffy man wedged into the corner of the boxcar. The old guy was obviously trying to make himself invisible. I grabbed James' arm and dragged him to the opposite far corner.

"There's a guy in here!" I whispered and pointed while trying to find a deeper shadow. James looked around and scanned the dark corner of the boxcar. The train passed an outlying building and a slice of light passed across the man.

"He's just an old drunk," James whispered, leaning close. He was probably right.

In his drunken fog, the old geezer wasn't sure if we were railroad police, muggers, or two guys who'd just climbed aboard his car. For the moment, he made no effort at further investigation, and neither did we.

The two of us flopped down on some crates, keeping an eye on the wino in the corner. I suddenly felt very tired and wished with all my heart that I was back in my bed. I also wished that James and his wild ideas would just leave me alone for a while.

"Well, wadda we gonna do now?" I asked again, sounding pretty perturbed about this new turn of events. "We going to chase them all the way to the coast?"

As much as I desired to be away from James and this grubby train, I knew that it was going to take both of us to wiggle out of this pickle jar. I looked over to see what he was concocting.

He was watching the guy lurking in the shadows, who I noticed as we passed a building with a porch light, was watching us back. He looked pretty old and drunk. Or, maybe so used to being drunk that he didn't know how to act any other way.

His head kind of lulled back and forth, like the wooden China doll my Aunt had sent me from the Far East. The doll's head was on a spring and Dad had put it in the back window of our Pontiac where her smiley head bobbed around . . . like a drunk in a boxcar.

"I got an idea," James quietly announced. "This train probably stops in Stevensville."

"Yeah, we can jump off and somehow get back home," I said, "to a nice whipping and grounding."

"Neal's not gonna whip ya because there's a sheriff's office in Stevensville, right?" James' mind was working.

"Yeah?"

"Well, we go right to the sheriff there and let him know what happened. He'll phone ahead and stop the train, and we'll be heroes," he added. He smacked me on the shoulder, happy with his new idea.

That was an idea that made sense. If the police were involved, maybe I'd not get in so much trouble, and I voiced my thoughts.

"If the police catch these guys and they drive us home, we'll pull up in police cars, right?"

"Yeah. That'd be cool," he said. I looked at him for a few seconds, thinking it over. Then I stuck out my hand and we shook.

Both of us felt better all of a sudden. I know I sure did. The idea seemed simple. Uncle Neal had to look at us as heroes. And as far as I could tell we wouldn't have to even get near those two gangsters in the car ahead of us.

Then the old wino began to uncoil himself and adjust to the swaying car. "You fella's got a drink?" the drunk interrupted loudly. He'd evidently come to the conclusion that we weren't the railroad police and weren't planning to roll him, and so decided to strike up a conversation.

"I like Four Roses, myself," he informed us. "Ya got a little Rosey on ya?"

"We don't have anything to drink, mister," James answered, trying to sound tough. The old guy didn't seem to care and started weaving over our way. The train was picking up speed, which caused its motion to become less predictable.

We'd both heard about hobos found dead along the tracks who'd fallen out the door while peeing, or simply getting up to move around. Most knew better than to venture around inside the swaying cars once they'd left town.

It was best to claim your spot and settle in for the haul, and share your bottle if you had one.

This desperate fellow, though, thought the risk of falling overboard worth the possibility that we might have something to share, and chose to weave his way through the scattered freight.

The only light came from the occasional passing of a building, and every time we caught a glimpse of the scruffy hobo, he was a few feet closer. When the lumberyard lights flashed his grizzled, unshaven face, he was practically on top of us, which was way too close for my comfort.

This guy looked as though he'd watched all the scary monster movies and put them together for his costume and appearance. In wino-world, he was probably right in style with his grimy overcoat and mismatched shoes.

I guess he was trying to be cordial when he stuck out his hand, for a shake or a drink, but we weren't about to touch his fingerless gloves and dirty hands.

His lopsided grin pushed up a bunch of wrinkles and exposed a row of yellow and black teeth. Scabs and wounds were scattered around his forehead and cheeks, and a few looked pretty fresh.

"Why, you're just a couple a pups," he observed with a happy scoff. His eyes had a strange way of rolling around in his head, making me wonder how he'd been able to notice what we were.

"Get outta here, mister," James barked. "We wanna be left alone."

"I'z here first, ya brats," The drunk scoffed and flopped down, practically landing on us. His smell wafted over me like a dank blanket. A combination of pee, booze, and years of human stink. He was grinning that off-balance grin and wagging his head back and forth at James and me.

"Where you feller's hail from, any hoo?" he slurred out.

I think he thought he was now one of our gang. The lights of a small farm revealed spittle forming at the corners of his mouth and suddenly reminded me of a living version of Harold and his misplaced features. Harold was probably this sorry drunk's pal, and on occasion shared a bottle or food scraps. The thought of putting my lips on anything this hobo's lips had touched made me retch.

Getting snatches of his weather-beaten face made me wonder if Harold's misarranged expression might have been what he normally looked like. I imagined Harold standing five feet away, grinning, with his teeth falling out, longing to get his cracked and bloody lips around a bottle of booze. The images were just too much.

* * *

Since coming to live with Gram and Gramps a couple of years back, I'd been firmly and repeatedly instructed to stay as far away from winos and hobos as possible.

"If you see one rummaging through the garbage or sleeping under the loading docks, you steer clear, ya hear?" were the instructions.

Whenever we saw one while over at the Co-op or the store they always grabbed the opportunity to educate me in the dangers of befriending a hobo.

"They're desperate folks, Calvin," Gram would say, hurrying me along if they were eyeing us. "They got no self-respect, and so they got none for others."

Gramps generally used a little more color and spice when laying down the law, if you know what I mean. Both of them, though, would always draw up short of telling me I'd go to hell or something while drilling it into my head that drunks, winos, and hobos were trouble.

* * *

They didn't need to go that far, because right now, finding myself sitting next to one of the devil's brats, as Gramps called them, made me want to crawl out of my skin and jump off this train. The fact that it was probably going thirty miles per hour wouldn't have mattered.

All that I'd been told came rushing in like a concentrated dose of Gramps' instructions when the geezer suddenly grabbed my knee. His horrific breath slapped me in the face when he laughed and squeezed hard. I jerked away at his touch, and so did James, I guessed.

"Get yer damn hands off me, ya stinkin' wino!" James shouted. Mostly, it was a yelp that burst from my mouth as I lurched to my right. The scabby fellow must have grabbed us both at the same time, thinking this was a grand joke having a couple of "pups" on board.

"Who ya callin' stinkin'?" he barked back at James, his jolly mood suddenly swinging the opposite direction. I heard a scuffle and a thud, and then saw James silhouetted in the open door. He was backing away.

"Ya little runt, come back here," the drunk barked. I scooted away myself, wanting some distance if the old guy planned on more knee squeezing. James though, hunkered low and stood his ground, his feet spread.

As captain of the Mud Lake Bulldogs defensive line, James had a qualified reputation for being tough. He liked the defensive line mainly because he could almost always wrestle his opponents to the ground and flatten the quarterback.

Our school was known for being pretty much unbeatable, thanks mostly to James' superior strength and physical creativity.

So, I knew if that old wino was looking to keep harassing us, he was bound to get a few more bruises.

I was starting to wonder if I wasn't having another "Harold" dream and turned my mind to trying to wake myself.

"Gram," I whispered. "Graaaam!" I said again, a little louder.

"Shut up, Cal," James snapped. "This ain't no dream."

Sometimes I was successful at waking myself out of particularly scary dreams by shouting out for Gram. I'd mentioned that fact to James one night while sleeping out?—?after a particularly bizarre dream about spacemen had made me wet my sleeping bag. I didn't tell him about the peeing the bag part and spent a miserable rest of the night.

"You bet yer butt it ain't no dream," the drunk growled. "You'll wish it were after I'm done workin' ya over."

He crawled to his feet.

"An' then I'm helpin' myself to yer Roses," he added with a sinister chuckle.

"We ain't got no wine," James repeated, in hopes that the man would back off. "Were chasin' some murderers."

The hobo laughed at that and started for James.

"Ain't nobody gonna come lookin' fer me after I murder you two pups," he hissed. "I'm invisible."

I clambered to my feet and got behind the skinny geezer. He didn't look all that able to do much damage. But we were a couple of kids, and no telling, he might have a knife of something.

I wished right off that I hadn't had that thought, because the next bit of light that slashed across the door revealed a slim blade in the wino's hand. I saw the instant fear in James' eyes too.

None of the offensive linemen James had faced ever held knives in their hands, so I could see it in his eyes that this changed things.

The old guy made a lunge at James, who jumped backward four or five feet. I circled around to the man's right side, allowing me to see them both framed in the large open door. I saw clearly when the old man made an arching swipe one way, and then back, that this was not the first time he'd used his weapon in a darkened boxcar.

But, skilled or not, James' speed made the wino look foolish and clumsy. James actually lunged back at the old man, which I found strange, but it took the drunk by surprise and he stepped back a little.

Then, realizing James was unarmed, the hobo combined both lunging at James and swipes with the knife, which threw him off balance. In that brief moment in time, I acted out of impulse and rushed the man.

I had yet to ever start in a football game; usually I only got to play if the score was ridiculously lopsided. But, all those hours of after-school blocking practice and pushing "the sled" across the field paid off, because that half-drunk hobo catapulted out the gaping door from the force of my cross block.

My own momentum almost launched me out as well, but James grabbed my shirt and yanked me back from the brink of crashing overboard. Unfortunately, my closeness to the door offered a perfect view of the wino tumbling in slow motion downward, through the gravel alongside the tracks.

I was struck with terror. I just killed someone! It happened so fast. It didn't matter that killing us was his plan. Not having any idea if he was dead or not, I assumed the worst.

"I killed him," I said low. I grabbed the splintery wood door jamb to steady myself, then looked up at James. "I killed that man."

"Geez, Cal!" was all James could say for the moment. I myself had no further words.

"He was gonna kill us," James finally said. "So I guess that's self-defense, right?"

I just looked at him and flopped on the floor. My stomach took over.

Puking was becoming a disgusting habit, I thought, as I lay on my belly and wretched over the side of the boxcar. So what that I'd pushed someone out the door of a speeding train car; I couldn't seem to keep things in my stomach. It didn't occur to me at that moment that perhaps I was getting into situations where anyone would lose their guts.

James just sat quietly next to me while I hucked and spit. I could tell that he was both humbled and struck with awe that I'd done what I'd done. We both knew that I'd probably saved both of our lives. Or at least saved us from getting cut up.

"Man, no one's gonna believe this story," James muttered mostly to himself. But, I heard him and turned my head around.

"You tell anyone about this, and I'll beat the juice outta you," I growled at him. It was not an idle threat either, and I was pretty sure James knew it. "That old geezer's probably dead. Or worse, lying there dying."

"Okay." Something in James' voice told me that he was supremely disappointed that this tale—or at least this part of it—would never make the rounds as far as I was concerned.

I held his eyes for a moment longer.

"I mean it," I muttered, feeling very weak and exhausted.

"I said okay," he assured me. "Okay?"

"Uncle Neal's belt'd feel like nothin' against goin' to jail," I added. I wanted James to know that this was serious; more serious than us sneaking out and jumping a train car to follow some gangsters. I hoped he understood. His face told me he did . . .

I crawled up and sat back against the wall and let my chin fall against my chest.

"I'd like to see you wup me, ya punk," James laughingly tested.

I didn't even look up. He could joke all he wanted; I wanted him to know that I'd give it my best shot if I ever heard about some kids—never mind who—who'd snuck out to chase murderers and ended up killing a wino in the process. It'd be just like James to change the names to protect the guilty just so he could scare the pee out of some wimps around a campfire. If anyone was gonna tell it, it would be me first.

James was not one for sympathy or a long attention span. After a few "whews" and "I can't believe you did that," he finally left me alone by the door. The October wind cooled my face and washed away some of the vomit and drama of the last hour.

While James poked around the dark boxcar, I considered what had gotten us into this mess.

Well, the first one was obvious—James and his never ending supply of snoopiness. He reminded me of a terrier we'd once had whose mission in life was to poke its nose into every danged hole in the ground.

If James hadn't gotten his hands on that dynamite and blasted the heck outta all the fish, we wouldn't have had to ditch it on the way back home. Which means we wouldn't have found Harold—er Jenkins—and we'd both be home in bed planning our next harmless project.

So, finding the body had been James' fault. One count against James. Then, I'd been the one wanting to leave Jenkins there in the bushes and forget it, or call Sheriff Stubbs. Another count against James. Wait a minute; I was the one who figured Stubbs wouldn't be any help. That's what got James thinking he needed to go investigate. Dang. One against me.

"Whose idea was it to sell Buster a look at Harold?"

I said into the darkness of the boxcar. I was pretty sure of the sequence, but wanted to make sure.

"Yours," James' voice replied from the dark. I thought for minute.

"Nooo, you saw him at lunch and said we should see if he'll pay to see Harold."

"Oh Yeah, yer right," James said blandly amidst some scraping. "I still think we could 'a made some money on that."

He stepped out of the dark and handed me a can with a tattered lid.

"What's that?" I said cautiously.

"Peaches. There's a whole case over there."

He slurped on his can. I took mine and sipped the juice. It tasted good. I was thirsty.

My mind went back to trying to figure out why I got in so much trouble. This was actually the first time I'd ever taken this line to think about things like this.

Usually, when I got home from some adventure, I was too tired to think about anything but dinner and bed, or too busy trying to come up with an explanation as to where I'd been, or why I was so bloody or muddy. It also struck me that I hadn't tapped on my own window a few hours ago; James had. There, another count against James. And, he'd been the one to dash off to follow the gangsters, against my objections. And then, jump on the train without my vote. Sometimes, when things look particularly outrageous, we'll take a vote. Which basically means James badgers me until I say yes. I do like a minute to consider what I'm getting into, and with this train business, I hadn't had any time to reconsider, let alone vote.

My mind was clearing and pointing to the fact that James was behind almost all the trouble.

"Why you wanna know about Buster?" he asked. There was a tone in his voice that suddenly concerned me.

James might be a blockhead about some things, but when it came to dodging responsibility, he was an expert. I think even if he was by himself and things went bad, he'd find a way to make it all right. I could hear it in his voice that he was winding up to make this my fault, or at least not his.

"Why you wanna know that?" he asked again, stepping back into view. "You pushed that geezer, not me."

"To save your life," I reminded him. I could tell he was suddenly on his guard.

"Wadda you thinkin' over here, Calvin Poag?" he asked as he sat down in the doorway.

"Nothing." I wasn't in the mood at the moment to discuss my thoughts.

"Yeah, sure you're not," he said and slurped out a peach half and popped it into his mouth. "You're thinkin' I got you into this mess, ain't ya?"

Like I said, James was smart. Just not about culture and stuff. I sipped my peach can, thinking how much I should let out.

"I was just thinkin' about that bum . . . and then Harold . . . and how it all got to this," I confessed. "He was somebody's son or dad."

"I knew it, Poag. You're thinkin' backwards again," he stated matter of factly. "Stuff happens and we get to go for a ride."

He suddenly took on that James-ish air of superiority. I knew I was in for a spoon-feeding of James-osophy.

"It's called fate. It's like throwin' a string in the air. It never lands the same way twice, and you can never predict how it'll land neither."

He started to go on, "Life is like a restaurant where you don't get to order, they just bring you something and that's yer dinner. You either eat it or go hungry.

That hobo you just heaved out the door, he was a bad man. And you saw that knife. He was gonna hurt us. When he did that, he chose to get hurt. None of us thought you'd be the one to do the hurtin' though."

James fell quiet for a bit. Then he took a different tact.

"Neither of us is religious, but both of us know that God saw what happened, and if that ol' wino hadn't gone out that door, one or both of us would have."

James was right about the wino and God and life being a restaurant.

That was pretty much James' normal way of looking at things. The trouble was he ate everything that they brought, every time. And most of the time, got me to dig in too.

* * *

We'd talked about this once before, after I'd nearly gotten killed under a train trestle. That was one of the first times I actually prayed.

It was last summer and we'd gone up the Little Salmon River to camp and fish. I knew the steelhead were starting to run and wanted to land me a couple. Under this old train trestle was a deep pool where those fish would lay up for a rest before pushing on upstream.

But, we were having a bad day and James wasn't interested, as usual. He was primed for something adventurous. That's about the time we heard the train off in the distance. James spun around and sat still, listening. He looked at me and grinned; that grin that told me a plan was hatching in his mind.

"Come on!"

He dashed off up the hill, kicking gravel and rocks down into the pool. I knew at the very least that was the end of fishing for a while, so I scrambled after him.

We could hear the train—way down the tracks—pounding toward the trestle. Which reminded me that once I'd heard an engineer telling someone that he didn't trust that old trestle. He always hit it as fast as he could in order to rush the drama of crossing it. So, I knew we were in for an adventure as we began to scoot out under the trestle.

By the time we'd wormed our way to about the middle, balancing on the giant tar-coated beams and posts, we were a sweaty, blackened mess. I had numerous slivers and cuts from trying to keep up with my nimble best friend, and the blood mixed with sweat made my hands slippery.

We didn't have time to really find a good safe spot, so when that monster roared over our heads we couldn't even shout at each other over the noise.

That engineer must have seen us because he blew his whistle right over our heads, just about splitting my ears.

"Oh God," I whispered, "don't let me fall."

I shifted my weight a little and felt more stable. Did God answer my prayer? Dunno for sure, but Gram and Gramps always said that prayer sure doesn't hurt.

After something like the train trestle adventure, an adventure that nearly ended with me in the rushing Little Salmon River, I would try to reflect on what happened. But, defining the line between fun and danger with James was just plain blurry and hard to see. If I did try and argue, that what we'd done might have been stupid or dangerous, he would swamp my boat with wild narration about the event from every conceivable view. If the line was fuzzy before the exploit, it was all but smudged out after sitting around the campfire that night.

James relived the excitement and drama, where I'd generally muse about the reasons and costs of such activities. Don't get me wrong, I liked doing stuff that was full of drama. I just didn't relax and turn it into a legend as fast as he did.

That night around the fire, with trout sizzling in the pan, I looked across the fire at him.

"What if one of us had fallen? I almost did."

"You know what my calling is, Poag?" James answered slantways. "It's to make you a man."

He laughed and I scoffed back, "Like you know."

"No, really. Men have to be tough and they have to take risks."

"They have to be smart too," I reasoned back.

"Heck yes, and I am smart," he said with confidence. "I look at a situation and work it out in my head before I do it. That's how I know I can do it."

I didn't say anything. Truth was I didn't have any idea what was in James' head when he did things like suddenly scramble out onto the train trestle or drop down ten feet into a black mine shaft.

"And I'm teachin' you how to do that too," he said, bringing his point full circle.

"What would you do if I hadn't been there?" I asked, genuinely interested. James stopped fiddling with the cooked trout and thought for a second. No one was going to stump him.

"Wouldn't a done it. Wouldn't a been any fun," he concluded.

"How come?" I asked, curious.

"Who'd believe me if I told 'em I scampered out onto the Salmon River Trestle when a train went over?"

"Me," I stated flatly. I'd been through too much with James for him to make up stuff.

"That's cuz you know me. You know I'm brave," he said like it was the most obvious thing in the world. "Not the other guys, though. They wouldn't. They'd say I was just full of it."

"Well, you are full of it," I jibbed. "I just don't see the sense in taking every risk that comes along."

"You sound just like yer dad, Cal. What's with that?" James was looking at me like I'd just grown horns or something.

"I dunno," I groaned. And I didn't. I was just kind of confused. I liked the stuff we did. Mainly afterwards, when the adrenaline had melted away and I was safe. Kind of like sitting around that fire all safe and sound, not having fallen off the trestle. That's when it seemed cool and okay . . . afterwards.

* * *

Not like right now, with a drunk hobo lying back down the tracks. Maybe dead. Or worse, broken and cold on an October night. I just didn't see an easy way out of this situation. We still had Dreggs and Ike to think about, which I really wanted to forget and just get home. However, that wasn't going to happen without James and me getting the police involved.

I was getting a headache and wanted to just go to sleep and wake up at Gram's, with bacon smells wafting up the stairs, and Uncle Neal having his first smoke on the porch, waiting to scold me for sleeping late and making his bacon get cold.

"Well, Uncle Neal, you're gonna have a mess to scold me about when you see me next," I thought.

Just then the train lurched and James crawled over to the door and peeked out. I wasn't anxious to see or know what was next. I figured we'd just get to the police somehow and they'd take it from there. That sounded pretty simple in my mind.

"Uh oh," James whispered. "They're gettin' off."

"Are we in Stevensville?" I said hopefully, but the lack of lights made me wonder if we might be too soon.

"No," James answered. "We're gonna have to jump off and follow 'em."

Oh great. I got up and started to crawl over next to James, but he tackled me and we rolled back into the gloom of the boxcar.

"Shusssh," he hushed. I turned my head so I could see the door, and sure enough, I saw Dreggs and the top of Ike's head bob past. Dreggs turned and glanced into our car. He didn't see us because he kept on moving.

"You didn't pee your pants did you, little man?" James asked with a smirk. I punched his shoulder and we got up and snuck over to the door. He called me that, little man, after our camping conversation up the Little Salmon, referring to his desire to make me a man. The part about peeing my pants, though, made me worry that he knew I'd wet my sleeping bag the night of my "spacemen" dream.

We cautiously peered out into the dim morning light. The train was still moving through the forest, which stood like a dark wall, and we saw Dreggs and Ike melt into the trees.

The train was still going pretty fast and I was about to object when James jumped and disappeared.

As I was flying through the air—just before I landed and rolled into a ball—I was thinking that James was more of a man than me. He just tackled life and moved on toward the quarterback.

That's when the world went black.

◇ **CHAPTER 6** ◇

Captured and Boiled

"The one thing I hate most about Amazon headhunters is that they always eat your legs first," I casually said to James.

It surprised me how calm I was considering we were surrounded by little grinning men with bones in their noses, sharpening long primitive knives. Our hands were tied to a post and our legs were extended out. Drool dripped from the natives' lips when they came over for a closer look. One was poking James' shoulder.

"He's testing to see if you're tender," I explained.

A photographer in a khaki vest with lots of pockets stepped up and took a few pictures.

He was draped with Nikons and used one to snap pictures of us. Then he shot a few more of the older natives eyeing our young plump legs.

"You done this before?" he said to me in an English accent.

"My third time," I replied. It struck me as strange that I also had an English accent.

The photographer aimed one of his cameras at James and clicked off a few shots. "It's his first, I'd say," he said.

I glanced over at James. He did look pretty nervous. He kept wagging his head back and forth between me and the hungry headhunters.

"You don't seem scared at all," James whispered.

"After a few times, you get used to it."

My breezy attitude toward having my legs amputated and cooked up in a stew was what first got my attention. One of the older headhunters was poking my legs with his knife and grinning. He had no teeth. Then, all the natives started poking our legs. On a table, I saw Tupperware right behind them. One headhunter, who looked like Groucho Marx, winked at me and said in a Jewish accent, "That's for leftovers tomorrow night." He pinched my legs once again for tenderness.

It was that pinchy feeling—just before they started cutting—that woke me up.

* * *

My head was pounding and when I opened my eyes, there was two of everything. I tilted my head a little and tried to get things to align and suddenly noticed what was causing the pinchy feeling . . . my legs were covered with red ants . . . a lot of ants.

"Ah!" I started brushing them off, but they were up inside.

I crawled to my feet and dropped my pants, instantly

dizzy from the effort. I sat right back down on the log I'd been propped up against and shook my pants.

While I slipped them back on things started to come better into focus. I looked around for James, but he wasn't anywhere in sight.

"Figures," I grumbled. "Whew, my head hurts."

I pressed my temples, trying to ease the throbbing. That's when I discovered a real sore spot. I put together that I must have taken a whack on the head and James dragged me into the trees. But, where was he? I stood up and steadied myself, thinking I might puke, again. "Oh no ya don't," I muttered, willing my stomach into submission. I started off toward the tracks.

The sun was peeking through the trees as I started heading out into the open . . . kind of wobbling along. When I reached the tracks I saw something sticking to a branch near the tree-line. It was a piece of James' shirt, and on the ground was a mess of footprints pressed into the October frost. It looked like a couple people had stopped for an early morning dance.

I suddenly felt very alone. Fear started to wrap around me and I ducked into a thicket of maples to think. It was hard though, my head was hurting so much.

"James is either following those two guys or they nabbed him," I whispered to myself. That made a shiver run up my spine and drew some pretty nasty pictures in my mind. I looked down the tracks, wishing a train would come chugging along right about then. Probably wasn't going to happen—this was just a secondary rail line and not used very often. So, no train for another several days. I had no choice but to follow the footprints and see where they led.

Once my vision cleared and the hammer in my head slacked off, I did pretty good at keeping to the tracks. I even found the place near a creek where they had stopped and done something. The needles were scuffed around and a stick broken. I had a drink of water and started off again.

It was just a little later that I heard Ike's voice and quickly hunkered down to listen. It wasn't too far ahead, so I crept in until I saw Ike messing with a fire. My heart jumped when I noticed James slumped against a tree with his hands tied together.

"Whew, he's alive!" I muttered to myself. But, where's Dreggs?

I squeezed myself into a thicket that offered a view, but hid me pretty well, and tried to figure something out.

What I wanted, of all things, was paper and a pencil. I always thought better when I could write out a plan. It was something that James and me did pretty often, when we were planning something big. I'd write while he talked. I instantly realized how stupid it was for me to want that right now. What I needed was to come up with a plan real quick; forget about writing it down. It wasn't going to be that complicated.

As I watched, I saw that James had a stick strapped to his leg and he moved kind of stiff when he tried to get more comfortable. Oh great. He's hurt, I complained to myself. That was going to slow us down.

Ike came over and looked at James' leg. He squatted down and made some adjustments to the rags that held the stick in place, which James seemed to appreciate.

I noticed a group of rocks off to the right of where they had him tied up. If I could get to the rocks, I might be able to get his attention.

Ike got up and shuffled back to the tiny fire and flopped to the ground. His back was toward me, so I slithered out of the maples and fell back into the shadows of the forest. I then circled around in a wide arch, and came up behind the rocks. It was even better than I thought. Dreggs and Ike had made their camp next to a small creek, which cooled my thirsty mouth. And the granite cracks formed slots, allowing me a good view of James. I had to crane my head, though, to see Ike and the fire. But Ike wasn't at the fire, he had his greasy head stuck under the water. James was watching him too and then scooted over to the creek and dunked in his leg.

When Ike came up blubbering and sputtering, he noticed James had his leg in the creek.

"Just coolin' yer heels, eh," he said.

"The swelling's killing me," I heard James explain. "You think you could loosen these ropes on my ankles? At least a bit?"

Ike looked around. "Dreggs won't like it."

"You can leave 'em on, just not so tight," James reasoned. "It's not like I can run off," he added with a tone of annoyance.

Ike nodded his head and untied the knot around his ankles and retied it looser.

"Oh, man. Thanks," I heard James say. "Ike, what's Dreggs gonna do with me, ya think?"

I couldn't see them very well, but Ike's slow answer didn't make me comfortable.

"I'm gonna look out fer ya the best I can, kid," he said. "You just behave, ya hear?"

Suddenly, Dreggs showed up out of nowhere, carrying a box. He immediately blew up at James and gave him a kick.

"Get yer little butt back to those trees," he hollered.

James obeyed the best he could, but Dreggs gave him another kick for added motivation.

"What're ya runnin' here, Ike? A free for all?"

"C'mon," Ike barked back. "He's just coolin' off the swellin' . . . nothin' wrong with that."

Dreggs took a swing at Ike, but missed on account

of the wooden box he was holding.

"The squirt was gettin' a drink," Dreggs barked.

"He's gotta drink, ya idiot," Ike countered.

"Is he still tied up tight?" Dreggs asked, not looking up.

Ike glanced back at James and then started over toward Dreggs.

"Yeah, course. I just caught 'im messin' around by the stream. What's that?" Ike pointed at the box.

"There's a cabin just up the hill. I helped myself to some supplies," he said with a sly grin. "I know how much you like beans 'n bacon."

Ike slapped his thigh and grabbed the little mess kit and started poking the fire back to life. Dreggs tossed him a chunk of bacon. "Get that sliced up and I'll get these beans open."

Pretty soon the smell of bacon frying wafted up into the rocks and actually brought tears to my eyes I missed Gram so bad. I had to turn away, not wanting to watch them eat it too. When I looked back, I could see the smells of home were having the same effect on James.

Those two pigs were shoving chow into their mouths like it was some kind of eating race. Dreggs noticed James watching and took a big bite of bacon and savored it as he chewed slowly.

"Ummmm. That's some tasty pork, there, Ikeiiii."

Ike threw a look over his shoulder toward James.

"What about the kid?" I heard Ike say, his cheeks pooched out with bacon and beans. He looked like a squirrel with a mouthful of nuts.

It worried me plenty that I couldn't hear Dreggs' response. All I saw was his evil glance. I was pretty sure breakfast for James wasn't part of Dreggs' plans, which kind of cooled off my stomach from its growling. I wished right then that I'd chowed down on that chop last night and not given it to Leopold. The thought of

Leo suddenly made me want to cry again and I had to suck it up a little.

"What else ya got in that there box?" Ike inquired, pulling it toward him. "Anything ta drink?"

"Get yer hands off that!" Dreggs scolded and whacked Ike's hand with a stick.

Ike snarled something I couldn't hear and jerked his hand back.

"I'z just thirsty!" he whined.

"I got somethin' for us. I just wanna play Santa." Dreggs grinned. He reached in and dug around and pulled out two bottles of whiskey and a cola.

"Whew hoo!" Ike yelped. He reached for one, but Dreggs held it back for a second.

He looked past Ike, toward James, as he popped the top of that cola.

"I'm thinkin' a nice cold coke-cola would go good with our whiskeys, don't you, Ike?" He was teasing James, and we all knew it. Dreggs got up and walked over and hunkered down next to James. Ike turned to watch, but didn't think Dreggs was all that funny. He wanted that whiskey and Dreggs still held the bottles.

Dreggs just looked at James and sipped that cola. "Ahhhh, that's some goooood pop."

He took another pull from the pop bottle.

I could feel my mouth starting to drool. I loved cola. Didn't matter which kind—Coke, Pepsi, Royal Crown. What I didn't like was Dr. Pepper . . . prune juice! That's what Gramps said was in it. Yuk.

"You drink that pop like it's water, Calvin," Gram would complain. "I should start making you buy it with your own money." She wasn't really mad because she still liked to make me smile and cold cola was the ticket for me.

"What I like," Dreggs started in again, "is cola and whiskey." He flopped down on the pine needles and opened one of the whiskeys. Ike came over with a worried look. He wasn't keen on any of that whiskey getting wasted on stupid games.

"What the hell're you doin'?" he demanded.

Dreggs just started pouring whiskey in with the cola until it was full. He took a taste.

"Ummmm, sweet with a little kick for fun."

"Quit foolin' around, Dreggs, an' let me have a sip a that."

Dreggs handed the bottle back to Ike, who didn't hesitate to slam back a few big gulps of the dark-amber fluid. Satisfied, he was more willing to let Dreggs tease their captive. James was eyeing Dreggs, knowing he was a loaded gun with a hair trigger.

"I'll bet you're thirsty, little feller." His voice had a nasty tone. "Well, let me tell ya somethin' . . . this here whiskey and pop gonna beat that creek water any day."

I could see in James' face that he was trying to be tough. I could tell, though, that Dreggs was making him nervous.

James and me once pinched some of his dad's bourbon and thought we'd have some fun on a camping trip. We both figured out pretty quick that drinkin' wasn't for us.

After we'd drunk about half that bottle, James fell in the river while showing off, and I tripped and sprained my ankle going to take a leak in the dark. That was all before we woke up the next morning with pounding headaches.

So, I could see that James wasn't keen for Dreggs' games.

"I ain't no doctor or nothin', but this here medicine'll help that leg feel better," Dreggs said as he roughly made James slurp down some of that whiskey and Coke. James spit it all out.

What a waste of a good Coke, I thought.

What concerned me was that Dreggs had slurped that bottle with his cracked and crusty lips, and now James was made to share off that same bottle. It made me wretch a little in the back of my mouth.

James sputtered and the concoction ran all over his face and shirt, but he chocked down some.

"Hey, ya little puke," Dreggs bellowed. "I see that you don't like whiskey and coke!"

Dreggs slammed James with the flat of his hand, sending him sprawling across the pine needles.

"Did ya see that, Ike? This kid's a brat," Dreggs complained, then burst out laughing. Ike nearly fell over laughing too.

"I seen it, Dreggs. That's what ya get for foolin' around with a mountain kid. He's just like we were at his age." He danced back to the fire, still giggling. "I think we should invite 'im into the gang."

Ike flopped back down next to the fire and took another long slug of whiskey.

"Ya little puke," Dreggs repeated, then spit at James as he walked away. James was dazed from Dreggs' cuffing, but got himself back sitting up. He just glared over at the two outlaws.

Finally, James asked the question of all questions: "What are your plans with me?"

Ike looked at Dreggs and Dreggs looked at James. Dreggs again burst into wickedly loud laughter and Ike followed along. They laughed in an evil, painfully sneering way. Then Dreggs got real quiet and Ike took his cue and quieted down too. The forest also went dead silent, like all the birds knew these two characters were about to decide what to do with James. Dreggs was again eyeing James and Ike kept glancing back and forth between James and Dreggs like he also sensed something different was up. I didn't like it, not one bit, and wished I was a better shot with a rock.

"The punk wants ta know our plans, Dreggs," Ike drawled out. Dreggs scoffed before speaking.

"It's real easy, little big man. You're too much trouble to pack along." He didn't say anything else for a minute. "I haven't decided whether to just leave ya, or just . . . leave ya."

Ike let out a snort and giggled. "That's a good one, Dreggs'er. Leave 'im, or leave 'im!"

Dreggs grinned at his comment and they both roared with laughter, coarse and hard, devilishly alive. Then, Dreggs just as sudden stopped laughing, flopped down on the ground, and slumped against a log. Ike looked startled, as if he had no idea which way the wind was going to blow next. So he followed Dreggs' lead and also collapsed against a log. The tension that filled the air a minute ago seemed to just evaporate and it wasn't long before both Ike and Dreggs were looking pretty relaxed from their whiskey. They were talking in that kind of drowsy way sleepy people do. I couldn't make out their voices, just that Dreggs would cast glances at James from time to time. Then, loud enough for me to hear, he said, "You keep watch a that kid while I catch a few." He sort of melted into a giant blob of grimy clothes with a greasy mop of hair on top.

Ike looked over at James and snorted. He also leaned back against his log and took another long pull on that whiskey bottle and tried to get comfortable.

I settled in and waited to see what would happen next and hoped for an opportunity to get James' attention.

You'd have to be an idiot to not know we were in a huge pickle jar. And after hearing those two thugs trying to decide what to do with James . . . get rid of him . . . or get rid of him permanently, it was obvious we were in way over our heads. I also realized this was one of those times we needed God's help. I'd been so busy trying to wiggle out of this mess that when the thought of prayin' popped into my head, it kind of took me by surprise.

Gram and Gramps were both big on prayin'. They were the first people I knew who prayed outside of church, and places other than grace at dinner, too.

"Calvin, you need to understand that God is everywhere, all the time. He's always watchin' over you. He's always available." Gram's eyes always got kind of wet when she talked like that. She'd tried one night to explain this everywhere all the time deal to me, but I just couldn't get it. It did kind of gnaw at me though when I knew I was up to something I shouldn't. The thought of God looking over my shoulder on a couple of specific occasions made me uncomfortable. But, I'd rather not talk about that.

I looked around again and thought hard about what to pray. Seems pretty obvious, Cal, I thought. So I put on my best serious expression and started in.

"God, this isn't exactly like praying at Sunday school, sittin' out here in these rocks 'n all. But, Gram says you're everywhere, all the time, so I guess that means you're right here too."

It kind of made me wonder why He'd be just hangin' around here in these rocks. I think that was when it started to make sense that God was with me all the time, everywhere. I'm the one who brought Him to these rocks. I just had a hard time talking to someone I couldn't see.

"I guess you know right off that James and me kind of messed up and got ourselves in a pickle jar," I whispered. "And, well, we need your help."

I couldn't think of anything else to say. I mean, that was it, why go on and on.

"Oh, amen . . . and thanks for bein' everywhere, all the time."

I don't know if it helped. I didn't really feel any

different. But, when I looked back around, there was Ike with his mouth hanging open . . . asleep, and Dreggs was also sawin' logs!

I knew this was the time to get James' attention.

He was watching them as well, twisting his wrists around trying to get loose.

The first pebble hit pretty close and kicked up a little puff of dust. He looked down at the pebble that seemed to fall from the sky, then casually looked around the camp with a funny expression. My second pebble hit him on the leg and he knew I was near. He finally found my face peeking out of the rocks and nodded slightly that he'd seen me. We started a simple conversation with sign language, mainly about getting him free, and he looked pretty anxious about getting on with it too.

A knot always crept into my stomach whenever it was do or die time. That's what James called the moment before jumping off into whatever adventure we'd devised. I knew he was referring to some old war movie where the guys were pinned down with machine guns spitting bullets over their heads and they needed to do something, or die sitting there. It struck me that that's exactly where we were right now. I could choose to sit in my hole in the rocks and do nothing, or climb down there and die in a hail of bullets.

It took a good fifteen minutes for me to reach James, what with being so darn careful not to disturb rocks, stay hid, and not crack a stick.

James was a little irritated that I'd been so careful. But, hey, better safe than sorry, I heard Gramps' voice say inside my head.

The knots on his hands and ankles were pretty easy to get loose. It was getting him to his feet without making a scuffle that was hard.

James leaned in so close I could feel the warmth of his breath in my ear. "It's do or die time, Calvin Poag."

"No kidding?" I replied. James' eyebrows went up in surprise, and he actually smiled a little.

He put some weight on his sprained ankle and winced, but I could tell he was determined to make something happen.

I started to back out of the camp, except James went the other way . . . toward Dreggs and Ike. What could I do? I couldn't holler, "What are you doing?" I had to follow. Besides, whatever he was up to now, he would need my help.

James moved slowly, his sprained ankle keeping him cautious. Near the fire was the little duffle I'd seen the men toss onto the train. James carefully picked it up and pulled out a short billy club. The kind used by cops. I instantly suspected this was the tool Ike had used to whack Jenkins, and the sight of it made my spine shiver.

James looked back at me and I could see in his eyes something new, and very dangerous. My eyes grew large and I shook my head, no. He nodded yes and turned back to the men.

James was standing closest to Dreggs, who was snoring softly. As James shifted his weight to get into position, Ike opened his eyes.

"HEY!" he yelled. Then Dreggs woke, looking groggy and confused. Not for long, though, because that hardwood billy club put Dreggs right back to sleep. He was out cold.

Ike jumped to his feet and rushed at James, who swung and struck Ike in the forearm, who then recoiled and stumbled backwards. I instantly grabbed a small log intended for the fire and took my batter's stance.

"I'll knock you into next week, Ike," James warned. "You can try for one of us, but my buddy here is a home run slugger!"

That wasn't anywhere near true, but Ike obviously wasn't prepared to test my swing. He rubbed his arm and crouched ready to defend himself.

"Look kids," Ike growled out as he looked back and forth between us.

"I was gonna help ya, I' told ya that," he said to James. "Dreggs, he's not trustworthy, but I was gonna help ya."

James moved out more into the open. He wanted swinging room and stood more squared up, the adrenaline making his ankle seem like an afterthought.

"Ya, just like you helped that Jenkins?" James snarled back.

Ike's eyes narrowed at the mention of old Jenkins. I too looked at James. That was a part of this story I felt pretty sure didn't need mentioning.

"Who's Jenkins?" Ike drawled out, trying to sound cool.

"You come near us and, I swear, you'll be in worse shape than Jenkins was. We both saw him! You aren't killing us like you killed him."

Ike's eyes were flicking back and forth between James and me, his mind working out his options. He then looked at Dreggs' big sleeping body and chose suddenly to dash off into the forest. This took both of us by surprise. We stood cocked and ready for action, but now had nobody to attack.

James straightened up and watched Ike vanish into the trees. He then looked around at me. "Guess he's heard about your batting average."

"Yeah, right. Come on!" I grabbed his arm to help him, but he shrugged me off and grabbed the duffle and started tossing in things, including the whiskey.

I watched the woods for Ike, and then we noticed Dreggs started to come around. James looked at me, and me back at him. He tossed me the billy club, which I held motionless.

"Cal," James whispered, indicating what I needed to

do.

I shuffled over and squinted, holding the club poised to strike. What had started as a dreamboat fishing trip was getting to be more and more like a nightmare charter cruise.

Dreggs looked up at me through foggy eyes and tried to move out of range. But, he didn't make it. He again slumped over unconscious from his second lump, freeing us to make for the woods as fast as James' gimpy ankle would allow.

But what about Ike? Was he lying in wait somewhere? Ready to nab us? Or had he really taken off for good? We had no idea what he was doing. All we knew was to run.

And I figured this was another good time for some praying. I figured because God was with me, all the time, He was now on the run with me; with both of us.

◊ CHAPTER 7 ◊

Spilt Beans

"I'll bet he's following us," I worried out loud for the umpteenth time. James ignored me. He was focused on not falling down, while I kept one eye searching the trees for Ike as we wove our way through the forest. To me, it just seemed logical that Ike would be following, looking for a chance to bushwhack us. James, though, had disagreed, reasoning that Ike had seen his chance to escape Dreggs and wanted that almost as much as we did.

"But, he knows we know about Jenkins," I argued. "Which, I'll say again, was a really bad idea to bring that up. I sure as heck wouldn't let a couple a runts get to the cops with that story."

I couldn't get over him blabbing about Jenkins. James was sorry for that and knew he'd raised the stakes for our getaway, but was not willing to come right out and admit it. He could be annoying that way.

When he screwed up, he almost always found a way to spin it around so it wasn't his fault. Or, he'd try and change the subject. When I saw that was the direction he was going, I generally just let it go. It wasn't worth a long argument.

"Just forget it," James said. "We need to put some distance between us and Dreggs."

He was adjusting the rags that held his splint and the pain was making him grumpy. The point was, we needed to make tracks anyway.

Even if Ike didn't come after us, we figured when Dreggs came around, he'd be gunnin' for James for sure. Neither one of us knew what he'd think about Ike being gone.

"Maybe he'll think Ike's off after us," I tossed out for discussion.

"Or you," James countered. "He probably can't figure out where you came from. But it don't matter who's after us, Cal, we gotta get to Stevensville and let someone know."

I could tell James was getting tired of me worrying. But, I just couldn't quit looking over my shoulder for Ike.

I learned while we worked our way back to the railroad tracks that I had taken a good bonk on the head when I landed and that James had dragged me off into the woods. Then he'd tried to find Dreggs and Ike, so he could track them. The trouble was, they'd found him first. He was a little fuzzy on the details, not wanting to talk about being tackled by skinny Ike. Like I've said, James had his pride when it came to tackling and stuff like that. I was able to fit together the skimpy puzzle pieces and had a pretty good idea of what happened.

"That's when Dreggs whacked my ankle. After I tried to make a break for it."

"So, that's why you whopped him good back there?"

I asked.

He just nodded. Layin' Dreggs out like he did had seemed out of character for James. He just didn't have anything to prove and didn't want a reputation. He liked playing football too much and fighting was a direct line to getting kicked off the team.

So, even though he could pretty much whoop anyone in the valley, he avoided fighting.

"That Ike fellow, though, he actually was tryin' to help me a little. He's the one who fixed up my leg so I could walk. Dreggs had whacked me so hard I couldn't hardly stand. I don't think he's following us, Cal."

James told me how Dreggs had cuffed him again for talking to Ike. Just before that, though, is when James learned they weren't really hobos. They were only hoboin' just to lay low for a while.

"I never heard what they were runnin' from," James said.

I also wanted to know more about Harold, or Jenkins, but James said Ike didn't bring up anything about that either. So, that was about all James had picked up before Dreggs put the screws on them for talking. Maybe James was right. Maybe it was Dreggs we really needed to keep an eye out for.

All we knew now was . . . get to Stevensville and the cops!

◇ CHAPTER 8 ◇

The Not-So-Great Escape

We must have gotten turned around with our directions cuz we come across a logging road that neither of us had seen before.

"Now, all we gotta do is wait for a truck or somethin'," James said, heaving a big sigh. He carefully eased down to the ground, really wanting to rest.

I was still worried about Ike and watched the woods like a hawk. I pointed toward a tight knot of trees down the road.

"Let's get in those trees over there, that way we can watch for a car and be hid if someone does suddenly show up."

James agreed and I helped him over to our new hiding spot. It was cool in the shade and we both settled in for a rest.

"I sure am hungry," James moaned when he got comfortable.

"That bacon those boys were fryin' up just about killed me," I said with a sigh.

"Oh man, me too. My stomach was growling so bad . . . and then that coka-cola and whiskey . . ." James' big chuckle told me it had gone straight to his head.

"Wadda ya think about Ike?" I asked. I just couldn't get that rascal off my mind. This was one time when I hoped with all my might that James was right, and Ike had high tailed it outta there for good.

"The way he jetted off makes me think he wanted to get away from Dreggs as bad as we did," James said.

"Looked that way to me too." I wasn't all that convinced, though. Something told me those two hoodlums were tied together somehow, a feeling I just couldn't shake.

* * *

We must have fallen asleep cuz the old faded Ford was pretty near when I realized what it was. I kicked James and he jumped awake.

"What! What's the matter?"

"I think it's a hunter," I pointed out.

I was right. Strapped across the hood was a four-point buck. I could see two hunters peeking out over the deer, probably happy about their kill, but not as happy as James and me.

I jumped up and sprinted from the trees. The car slowed when they saw me waving, and the guy in the passenger seat reached around to get the back door. When the car stopped, and the passenger looked back, it was Ike! And he was holding a 30-30 bolt action rifle.

He quickly chambered a round and pointed it at the driver, who was as shocked as me. Ike reached over and switched off the car and jumped out. That's about the time James came hobbling out of the trees and his eyes just about popped out of his head.

"Need a lift, boys?" Ike blurted out with a smirk. The sinister, satisfied grin on his face said that he thought he'd won after all. My gut had been right. He just hadn't come out of the woods on a dead run like I thought he would.

Ike turned back to the driver. "Okay Pops, get out!"

The driver was an old guy, dressed in a hunting outfit. He slowly climbed out.

"Sonny, you're diggin' a real deep hole here," he said to Ike from the other side of the car. I guessed if the shootin' started, he wanted something between him and this crazed hitch hiker. Even if it was his car.

"Shut up and take off yer clothes."

"What?" the driver asked, sort of befuddled.

"You heard me, Pops. Drop 'em!" There was a long stare down that made me think the old guy might get blasted if he didn't drop his drawers.

"Your choice, Gramps," Ike warned. "Yer pants or a big nasty hole in yer chest." Ike leveled the rifle at the old man and he reluctantly started stripping down.

James was holding the duffle bag and started to reach in. I figured he was going for that little billy club, but Ike also noticed.

"Hey, gimme that bag, kid!"

James pulled out his hand and tossed the duffle over to Ike.

"Don't ya know a 30-30 trumps a wooden billy club any day?"

Ike laughed as he scooped up the bag and tossed it into the backseat of the car. That's when Ike noticed that the old hunter had his clothes off. He looked pretty ridiculous standing there in only his underpants and undershirt. I didn't laugh. It wasn't funny. It was kind of pathetic, actually.

"Toss 'em over, and the hat." The man did as he was told. "Now, get over there." Ike indicated a grove of trees well off the road. The man hesitated.

"Mister, you blast me or these youngsters and you'll spend the rest of your days stampin' out plates. Or worse, I recon," the old hunter said.

"I been there. It ain't so bad. Got three hots and a cot," Ike answered with a mean chuckle and then grinned. "But I ain't plannin' on doin' any more stampin'." Ike waved the gun and the old man reluctantly shuffled over to the trees, keeping an eye on us and Ike.

"Now, which one of you can drive?" Ike snapped back at us.

Well, that was easy; James was the only one between us who could drive.

"Me, I can drive," James stated flatly.

There was something about the way he answered that sounded like the wind was leaving him. I guess I can't blame him, though. Having a known murderer pointing a gun at ya would take the wind out of just about anyone. I was starting to feel pretty flat myself. It was kind of like being thrown into a room and the door locked. Up 'til then you have hope that maybe you can escape. But, once inside and the door locks, that hope leaves.

Ike, standing there waving a cocked 30-30 at us, was kind of the same thing. What could we do? Run? Even if he was a lousy shot, James and his hobbled leg would be pretty easy pickin's.

"Get in," Ike growled. "And I don't have ta tell ya, but if ya try any monkey business . . ." Ike fired off a round into the air. "No one'll even care that a gun went off? . . . huntin' season 'n all," he said with a nasty grin, and chambered another bullet.

The bullet sound reverberated around in the forest for a second, making me hope some nearby hunter would come a runnin' to see what the guy got. Hunters were funny that way. James and me both looked at each other, then James hobbled around and climbed into the driver's seat. Ike motioned for me to take the passenger side and climbed in the back with his gun handy.

The deer was so big neither of us could see very well out the front, which made James' peddle work difficult.

He turned the key and the engine cranked and cranked, but wouldn't start. He turned off the key and tried again. Still nothing happened but the growl of an old engine that wants to sit and rest rather than go anywhere.

"Ya gotta hold down the gas," the old hunter said from across the road. "It floods."

"What'd he say?" snapped Ike.

James didn't answer, he just tried again, with the gas held down and the car soon started.

We lurched off down the road about a hundred yards and stopped.

"What's wrong with you?" Ike barked.

"My ankle! It's killing me when I shift!" James said, a little too testy for my tastes . . . with Ike armed in the back seat.

"You two switch places."

"But, I can't drive," I complained. I also thought it a good time to start being more polite.

"Well, you're gonna learn, ya mouthy little runt."

We climbed out. I had a brief thought of dashing off into the woods. But, leaving James as Ike's single hostage made that idea fizzle fast, and so I wandered around the car and climbed in.

I noticed the old hunter standing out in the road, probably wondering why we'd stopped, but also glad he was alive. All he'd be when he got home was embarrassed. I'd be skinned alive and hung on the barn for the whole town to see. If we made it home.

Another thought popped into my mind that maybe I should just convince Ike that I'd make a great partner. Kind of an apprentice gang member. That way, I wouldn't have to get blistered by Uncle Neal's belt. He'd probably use the extra wide belt he saves for just these special occasions. I think I actually groaned out loud seeing both sides clearly. I was dead either way.

"Put the clutch in," James instructed. "And then give it some gas."

I obeyed and revved up the engine.

"Easy, not so much gas!" Ike yelled. "You'll blow us all up!" That suddenly didn't sound like such a bad idea. I let off the gas and eased out the clutch. The car started to move forward. I knew what to do . . . I'd just never been given the chance.

Most of the kids around the valley knew how to drive. If it wasn't tractors, it was farm trucks. By the time they were ten years old, many of them were even allowed to come into town on short errands to the store or feed co-op. Gramps hadn't taught me because we lived in town. Uncle Neal saw no reason either and I didn't press the point.

Ike was getting nervous. He kept looking around. I could tell he wanted to get on the road and capitalize on his new transportation.

"You gotta shift, kid!"

"Okay, put in the clutch and let off the gas at the same time," James instructed, "and then shift."

James moved his hand around to indicate what he meant. I worked the clutch and let off the gas. Then James just reached over and shifted the stick.

"I can do it," I snapped.

"Okay, okay. I was just tryin' ta help." James backed

off.

An idea suddenly popped into my head that I needed to let simmer, and that was starting an argument with James. Used in the right moment, it could create a diversion. I reached over and slugged him on the shoulder. I hoped he'd get it.

"Hey," James growled.

"You're always doin' stuff for me!" I snapped. This was so far from the truth that I was sure he'd get it. "You won't even let me drive! You never let me drive at home either! So just keep your hands off!"

I shot him a nasty look. I wish I'd been able to snap a picture of the look of shock on his face. I could almost see the wheels turning.

"Yeah," Ike chimed in. He'd taken the bait, at least nibbled on it. "Let little brother here drive for once."

James threw up his hands in mock submission. "If Dad finds out you been drivin' . . . what with your seizures and all . . ."

Seizures? What seizures? I've never had a seizure in my life. Where's this gonna go? Brother, could James take the ball and run. He really should be playing offense in football, the way he plowed right through when he had the chance.

"I guess we won't tell him then," James went on. "We're gonna be in so much trouble anyway when we finally get home!"

"Seizures? What seizures?" Ike wanted to know.

"He doesn't like to talk about 'em, Ike. So just drop it, okay?"

"I ain't droppin' it! What seizures?!"

I started to answer, but James was making an end run and going for the goal line. How could I stop him now. He might score.

"Well, when he gets scared . . . it's something to do with his adrenal glands."

Oh boy, here we go . . . James and his medical terms.

"What's a drenal gland?" Ike asked, suspicious.

"A-drenal. It makes adrenaline. You gotta shift again," James directed toward me. He could tell I had no clue where to put the shifter next. "Up and to the right."

"I know where ta put it," I grumbled.

I executed a pretty good shift to third and we picked up speed. Because the deer was blocking my view, we were weaving all over the road, which was making everyone nervous. Even me. James decided to continue explaining my seizures.

"That gland pumps too much juice into his system and he goes, well, kind of crazy."

I shot James a dirty look. This business about me having a seizure had gone far enough.

"That's not funny!" I seriously hoped I wasn't going to have to actually have one, not knowing what a seizure looked like. I had a sinking feeling it was something like the spaz attacks all us kids did sometimes. The classic spaz attack was generally performed to laughter; so I instantly imagined myself on the ground with my face contorted, my arms curled up to my chest, and drool pouring out of my mouth. It also sounded like a great time for Ike to blast me out of my misery.

I wanted desperately to get James' attention to let him know that I was feeling great. At the very least, I wasn't feeling seizurely.

"Adrenaline controls the way we react to fear. Like when I clobbered you in the arm. Adrenaline made me do it."

Oh, man, James was on a roll. He would have to bring that up.

"Which, because of my adrenal gland working so well, I want to apologize for that."

I caught a glimpse of Ike in the rearview mirror. He

was looking at James like he was a Martian.

"Kid, you're crazy. A-drenal gland my butt."

"Really, Cal's Gramps was a vet. He told me about it."

"Shut up, ya hear?" Ike snapped.

"All I'm sayin' is, Cal could go kind of crazy if you get him too excited."

"Wadda mean, Cal's Gramps? I thought you two were brothers." Ike was suddenly looking extremely suspicious.

"We are. Cal's adopted. But it's his Gramps on his mom's side."

James blinked to add a touch of charm after wiggling through that hole. It was a classic Lucy Ricardo look and Ike seemed to buy the yarn and settled back, like a befuddled and foolish Charlie Brown.

There was a little truth to his story. Gramps had been kind of a veterinarian, although not professionally trained. His dad had been a vet and Gramps had picked up enough from him to keep the tradition alive, and a lot of animals too.

After a few miles I'd gotten the hang of keeping the car pointed straight and was going about forty miles an hour when Ike put the screws on my driving.

"It's a logging road, Cal, not a race track," Ike stated while chewing the sandwich he'd found in the hunter's stuff. He'd also found some chips and coffee. I generally didn't drink coffee, unless it was offered on a cold morning while fishing. I then pumped it full of milk and sugar, and it tasted pretty good.

Right now, with me thinking about eating the steering wheel, and Ike hoggin' what little food he'd found, it was really torturing me and James. We were both growling in the gut and the smell of tuna and pickles was almost too much. He even let out a perfectly tuned belch and laughed about it.

"Umm,um. That was perfect. Ya know, my momma used to make tuna sandwiches just like this. But, she'd put a little pepper sauce in there, and man oh man . . ."

I couldn't stand it. I thought about crashing the car into a tree. At least we'd be in the hospital where we'd get some food.

I rolled that idea around a little, but soon ditched it when I realized James and me would probably get hurt. The picture of us poking through the windshield lost its appeal pretty quick.

I glanced over at James to see if I could detect anything that resembled a plan, but his head flopped down on his chest. I couldn't believe it . . . what a time to take a nap! With a 30-30 pointed at our backs!

"Calvin, ya want some chips?" Ike said kindly.

"Yeah. Thanks."

"Too bad. They're all gone!" He burst out laughing. And James popped up and blinked his eyes. He looked surprised that he'd dozed off. He blinked and looked over the seat.

"What's the plan here, Ike? We need to know the score."

"Oh you do, do you? The score is, you two pups are my ticket outta this tree-lined armpit of a country. That's the score, pal!"

I could see him settle back in the seat with a satisfied smirk.

"What about Dreggs? You just gonna leave him up here?" James was fishing for anything.

"Oh, you wanna go back and get Dreggs, do ya? That'll be fun, don't ya think?" His voice took on that angry edge it had earlier. I wished James would just quit poking at Ike.

"Dreggs," Ike scoffed. "He thought he was the brains. It was his idea to bring Jenkins in on the plan. Like we needed a wino to help hold up a bunch of geezers in a grain co-op."

Ike pulled out a cigarette and lit it. He sucked on the smoke and blew it out.

"I saw right through that Jenkins guy from the start."

I watched Ike in the mirror staring out the window . . . thinking.

Then he added, "When I caught 'im skippin' outta camp with our dough, I nabbed 'im and whopped it outta 'im."

Ike puffed on his smoke and thought for another minute.

"Didn't mean ta send 'im off to his maker, though. That was basically an accident. Dreggs was just mad that I was right and took it out on me. That's when I figured I needed to put some ground between us." He smiled. "You two came along at just the right time. Real convenient."

"So, wadda ya gonna do with us? Ya can't just kill us . . . we're kids, Ike. Ya kill a couple of kids and they'll fry you in the electric chair." James was trying to sound just a little too tough again.

"Yeah. I've heard your hair catches on fire and your eyes boil and pop," I added. I'd read about what happens to folks when they juice 'em up in the electric chair and thought my knowledge on the subject might help Ike decide to let us go?. . . unharmed.

"Yeah, I heard that too, Cal. Don't really care, though." Ike's casual tone and grin really made me nervous. He pulled deep on that cigarette and blew out real slow.

"I ain't decided just yet what I'm a gonna do with you two. But, when I do, I'll be sure to let you kids know."

Ike snapped his head around.

"Hey, pull up that little road back there. I gotta take a pee."

I got the car turned around and parked up the little logging road Ike had spotted. He made us get out and stand apart, with our pants down around our knees, before he walked off to do his business.

I hadn't peed in hours and decided I might as well take the opportunity. James was thinking the same thing. But, we were so far apart that we couldn't do any talking.

When I was done, I looked at Ike, who was still busy, and I did a speedy spaz attack for James, and he actually snickered. Me too. It felt good to share a quick joke. Ike heard our giggles and yelled out.

"Hey, you two cut it out!" He walked back over. "Ya think this is funny?"

"No sir. James just has a crooked . . . well, you know," I said.

"James is it? Well, James, you and your brother, Calvin, load up," Ike sneered.

James glanced at me for telling his name. I just looked back and shrugged.

"He likes to be called Jimmy, Mr. Ike." It took all my strength to hold in a big laugh. I knew I was dead meat when James got a hold of me. I also knew I was going to be having a spaz attack sometime real soon. It would probably be the only way to balance the books.

"Jimmy, eh? My little brother's name was Jimmy."

The thoughtful way Ike mentioned that made me wonder what happened to Jimmy. "He was the first person I killed. When he was twelve. Hated 'im, Jimmy!" He spat out the name like a nasty hairball.

I was suddenly very sorry I'd brought that up.

After about another twenty minutes, we hit a main road. The sign said, "Stevensville 15 miles." I just sat there, waiting for instructions. James had lost some grit too after the Jimmy story.

Ike was obviously thinking things over, and sat still

for a few minutes, smoking and thinking.

"If we go to Stevensville, you could get another car and skip outta town," James offered.

"Yeah? And you and your little brother wouldn't go right to the sheriff, would you?"

"Uh ah." We both shook our heads, no.

"Yeah right. Shut up you two and let me think."

"We always write down our plan, so we get all the parts right," I offered. "Ya wanna write down your plan? We could help."

Ike looked at me like I was crazy. "Turn the car around, Calvin, and go back up that two track."

$\Diamond$ **CHAPTER 9** $\Diamond$

Return of the Hunter

Once I got the car stopped, I decided to try out a plan I had.

"Mr. Ike, is there some TP back there?" I let my question hang, hoping he'd get the drift.

"What if there is?"

We had just pulled the deer off the hood and he was lounging, having another smoke. He suddenly got the picture. Maybe it was my intense look that clued him in to my predicament. Anyway, he let me grab the half roll of TP and I started to dash off into the forest.

"Hey, take off yer shoes before you go trottin' off out of sight."

For a criminal, Ike was kind of smart. He took precautions when it came to not letting me or James skip out on him, even if James was in no condition for "skipping."

Ike had the gun, but he wasn't taking any chances.

He'd used the deer's rope to hobble James' arms so he could only open them about sixteen inches and made sure that the billy club was lashed to his own belt.

Once I was by myself, I realized that my plan wasn't going to work. Ike was sticking by the car and had James close by.

What bugged me later, when I looked back, was that if James had managed to be in my situation—hunkered down by himself—he would have been planning something. Me, I was worrying over Gram and Uncle Neal, wondering what they were thinking. Certainly, by now, they'd be the real ones who were worried. Gram was probably scared and crying.

Someone would have found our bikes behind the co-op, and maybe even Sheriff Stubbs had made it up from Salmon. They might even be working on a search party. The thought of folks out combing the forest and railroad tracks suddenly gave me some hope.

When I came tiptoeing back to the car, and put on my shoes and socks, I was feeling a little better. Maybe everyone would make such a fuss about James and me being found alive, saved from the hands of desperate men, they'd forget to whip the hides off of us. My spirits were rising. All we had to do was stay alive so we could get rescued.

When I rounded the front of the Ford and saw Ike and James deep in some kind of planning, I froze for a second. What's James doing? Helping Ike? Me and him were supposed to be working out our own plan, not helping these murderers. What got me was James had that kind of crazed look in his eye he gets when he thinks a plan's really coming together.

"We got to find a different car and get some food," James was saying. Ike wore a kind of sneer that I think was supposed to be a smile.

He looked up at me and said, "Yer pal here's got

some good ideas."

James saw me and instantly wanted my opinion.

"How we gonna get into town without being seen, Cal?"

"Heh . . ." I stammered.

I'd thought James was just trying to keep Ike from blasting our brains out from between our ears when he'd offered "to help." But, here he was drawing in the dirt, moving pine cones, trying to plan out Ike's escape. I flopped down and decided to just jump in. I took charge and James looked positively shocked.

"Forget going to town. We need to get away from town and ditch this car. That old hunter will get picked up pretty soon and this car's a target." I stopped to think. "What we need is a map; a Forest Service map, and figure out the really back roads that can take us over the mountains and down to the gorge. But we need to wait till dark and travel at night."

I'd decided that maybe if we could help Ike escape the state, or at least the county, he'd feel safe enough to let us go—without filling us full of holes first.

I looked right at Ike?. . . something I'd not liked doing up 'til then.

"Once you hit the Columbia Gorge, you can take either highway. You got the Washington side or the Oregon side," I said, trying to sound cheery, like he had so many wonderful options. "And there's lots a little stores and gas stations all along the way."

You can rob 'em all, or do whatever you want, I thought.

Ike just smiled and puffed on his cigarette.

I suddenly remembered he'd mentioned wanting to get to Mexico. I prayed Ike would forget that he'd said that. James and me knowing where he was heading would be dangerous. I also prayed that James would hit on the same thought. Sometimes his mouth would kick into gear before his brain had a chance to put on the brakes; something I'd learned to do about two days after Uncle Neal elbowed his way into my life. Taking my time answering Neal's questions became a science for me.

"Ain't you two the couple a bank robbers," Ike finally said with a sly tone. He sat there looking at us looking back at him.

"Wadda we eat? That sandwich didn't put much of a plug in my tummy."

Too bad, Ike. I thought. Food sounded good to me too?. . . especially the "we" part. It meant he wasn't going to kill us. At least not right off. Of course, they always offered the prisoner a "last meal" in the movies. Hmm, my last meal, I silently asked myself. What would I eat? A Yaws hamburger would be good. With extra pickles. And fries. The fat fries with the skin still on. Not those skinny ones that get cold. You get more with the skinny ones, but I don't like cold fries. Ah, I sounded like Uncle Neal! I shook off the thoughts of food. I could feel my mouth twitch and start to water.

"We gotta get some food before anythin' else. You two gang members think a somethin'. . . I gotta go . . . where's that TP, Cal?"

I pointed to the car and Ike sauntered off, leaving James and me alone for a few moments.

Ike barked over his shoulder, "And, no plannin' yer escape! This gun'll shoot darn near a hundred yards. You two just figure out where we can get some steaks and taters . . . with butter. I like lots of butter! Never get enough butter in the joint!"

Ike was still grumbling as he slipped off behind some bushes.

"How about hot fudge sundaes too," I muttered.

James snickered, and then moaned at the wonderful thought of hot fudge. I was sorry I'd mentioned it. My stomach also groaned.

Ike was a slow-goer, so it gave James and me some time to work out a few things. One of which was that I was feeling just fine and not planning on having any seizures.

"I thought that was pretty smart," James explained. "If we need to create a diversion, you could just go into a conniption and draw Ike's attention."

"Yeah, right. And you, the one-legged hero," I replied. I didn't mention that it would be hard for me to be of any help while flopping around like a grounded fish.

We had just started to try and figure out our next meal plans when an old rattly truck tore past on the main road. We heard it skid to a stop.

"I hope that's the cavalry comin' to our rescue," James wished out loud.

"Me too," I agreed.

We sat frozen and watched. Then, the driver ground the gears and an old grubby Chevy truck backed up and sat there for a second. Then it turned and started up the two track road.

I glanced back toward the bushes to see what Ike was doing, but he was laying low.

We both wanted to jump up and wave our arms. But the way this day had gone, neither of us was ready to jump up just yet. I looked over my shoulder again, and from where Ike was positioned, he could easily blast the ears off whoever that was nosing around, or us too if he wanted.

I could feel my heart really pick up speed thinking that this could finally be the end of this day. I'd had enough of being hungry and having a gun pointed at me.

Then I saw who was behind the wheel of that truck. So did James because he let out a low growly groan. It was Dreggs, and seated beside him was the old hunter in his undies!

"Uh oh," was all James could say. He knew we'd been playing with the big dogs the minute he'd been nabbed and clubbed in the ankle. So, when the biggest dog with the biggest teeth suddenly showed back up, we knew this day had gone from horrible to horribler.

"You boys okay? The old hunter hollered as he jumped from the truck. All we could do was nod meekly. He noticed that our eyes were glued to Dreggs, who looked pretty peeved off as he walked around the Ford and glanced inside.

"Where's that weasel, Ike?" Dreggs asked, more like a growl.

Neither me nor James could speak . . . I think we were both in shock. But James pointed toward the trees. That's when the shot blasted the headlight out of the Ford.

"Dang!" shouted the hunter, ducking for cover. Dreggs bolted back to the truck and grabbed a shotgun that was in the back window. James and I scrambled over near the Ford and tried to hide. I could hear a clicking sound from the bushes where Ike was hid.

I looked around and saw Ike making for the trees, trying like mad to pull up his drawers. A loud pop from Dreggs' gun sent Ike to the ground with a high-pitched yelp. Ike jumped up and tried to keep going. His rear end and back had little red marks from where the bird-shot had pelted him. I looked back at Dreggs who had another bead on Ike.

"Don't make me blast you again," Dreggs yelled. "Now get your peppered butt back over here!"

Ike stopped and turned around. James and me suddenly realized what a terrible shot Ike was, and that he'd only had one bullet left in the 30-30. All Ike had succeeded in doing was stir up the hornet's nest that lived inside Dreggs. Now, Ike was in the same pickle jar as us, and he started right in trying to talk his way out.

"Hold on there, Dreggs. Don't shoot until you hear me out!"

Ike was trying to get his pants up, but the birdshot made it all sting. "Dang you, you really blasted me good." He tried to sound amused, like it was all some great joke. I could tell by the shake in his voice that if he hadn't done his business before the shootin' . . . he'd be doin' it now!

As Ike waddled back into the little clearing, he tried to keep the Ford between him and Dreggs, just in case Dreggs decided he needed to put another round of shot in him.

"Lay that gun on the ground and step clear, Ike!" Dreggs shouted. "One a you boys grab it, and don't try anything funny."

Dreggs was not taking the light-hearted bait Ike was dangling out there. He was all business.

I looked at James, knowing it was me who was elected to grab the rifle. I slowly came out and inched my way to where Ike had laid it against the Ford.

That stupid Ike; if he hadn't tried to shoot Dreggs, he could have talked his way outta this easy. Even I knew that. His lousy aim and an itchy trigger finger was probably going to get him killed. I opened the bolt in the rifle and showed Dreggs that it was empty and laid it back down.

"You know this rascal?" the old hunter asked Dreggs, indicating Ike.

"You shut yer trap, Gramps," Dreggs ordered.

Ike cautiously slumped against the Ford and pasted a silly smile on his face. I could tell that those number 9 BB's were stinging his rump like little hot needles. James and me just laid low watching, ready to run for cover. We figured Dreggs had enough on his hands for a few minutes trying to figure out Ike's story. Ours would be easy. We had an excuse. Not that it mattered.

"Those two runts know about Jenkins?" Ike blurted out right off the bat.

"Oh man," I heard James groan.

Dreggs looked around at us quickly, his brain working overtime. After all, this was a lot to process for an idiot such as Dreggs, who probably had a pounding headache to boot.

"Wadda you talkin' about?" The words drooled out of Dreggs almost like syrup. When I looked up, his eyes were drilling holes right through me.

"Yeah," said Ike. "They found 'im right where . . ."

"Shut your pie hole!" Dreggs barked.

He stood there a second, thinking. "Come 'ere." He indicated for Ike to follow him off a ways. Ike did, but wasn't too keen. It hurt as he hobbled.

"That one's a vet," Ike said, throwing over his shoulder toward me. "Maybe he could get these BB's outta my butt."

My eyes flew open. How Ike had gotten that idea—that I was a veterinarian—was obvious he was a lousy listener, as well as a horrible shot! James looked at me. I could almost see the visions he was having of me digging around inside Ike's back and other parts, for #9's. I was having them too, and it wasn't pretty. I felt my face pinch up. I looked at James and his face was also scrunched into a concerned expression.

"I know what that feels like," he muttered under his breath. "One slip and Ike could reach around and kill ya!"

We both knew what he was talking about. I ended up digging out a few BB's one night after a particularly wild idea and adventure. But that's another story.

"And we got nothing that even resembles medical tools," I muttered back.

While Ike tried to bob-and-weave his way out of

Dreggs' sights, I couldn't get outta my mind the images of Ike's bloody rump?up in my face. What made me even more worried was that I knew how to do it.

I'd helped Gramps last year do the very same thing for a guy's hunting dog who'd accidentally gotten in the way of a 12 gauge. At least that's how the hunter told it when he came over for help.

I could tell by Gramps' "uh huhs" that he didn't really believe him.

"Didn't train his dogs ta not range out so far," he said when he showed me how shallow the BB's were.

"A 12 gauge would've put these pellets right through this pup if he hadn't been fifty yards out." Clink went another pellet into the pan. He'd let me fish around for one, but then I flopped over on the floor and fainted.

I could feel my head starting to lift off my shoulders as I thought more and more about doing this medical procedure on Ike. James could see that I was starting to feel dizzy.

"Ah, can Cal here get a drink of water or something?" James hollered over to Dreggs and Ike. Ike said something and Dreggs just waved that I could.

"You stay where you are, Gramps," Dreggs pointed at the old hunter.

All James could find was the whiskey he'd pinched when we escaped from camp. He handed it to me and I hesitated. I took a pretty good pull off the bottle and swallowed hard. Instantly my throat was on fire and I sputtered and coughed. I looked up and my eyes were all teared up. The stuff hit my stomach and felt like I'd swallowed a red hot rock. Right after that I felt it creep up to my head and neck and I had to give my head a quick shake.

"Whew," I said.

James snitched a little too and had almost the same reaction. He looked at the hunter and wanted to hand the bottle to the old man, but decided not to risk it. He shrugged and set it down.

We couldn't really hear anything the two criminals were saying, but whatever Ike was selling, Dreggs must have been buying because he seemed to cool off a little. If you could ever call Dreggs cool. He looked like someone who was born mean. If he'd been a fish, I'd of thrown him back.

"You boys okay?" the hunter asked, keeping his voice real low and not exactly looking at us. We both nodded, but he could see we were pretty scared. He leaned against the fender of the old pickup and looked pretty tired.

"Were ya from?"

"Mud Lake," James whispered back.

That was the end of our getting-to-know-the-old-hunter because Ike and Dreggs had reached a truce of some kind and started back our way. That's when I suddenly piped up.

"I wonder if this old guy has a tackle box?" I'd directed my question more or less at Ike, but it was like someone else had said the words . . . someone else inside my head who was using my mouth. Whoever it was kept on coming up with ideas.

"If'n he does, he might have some tweezers." I blinked and smiled a little funny smile. Ike just looked at me. So did James and the old hunter.

"I could give it a go, diggin' out those BB's, I mean."

I really wanted to scream out that I had no idea how to do that kind of thing, but my mouth had gotten away from me and there was no turning back.

"He's watched his Gramps pull out BB's before," James added. He decided to leave out the part about him getting a few in his rump. I thought about bringing that up, but decided against it.

"Watched?" Ike growled, sounding unconvinced.

"Well, he let you do some, didn't he, Cal?" James asked and nodded, trying to get me to nod too. I could feel my head bob up and down like that China doll in Dad's old Pontiac window.

"Well, whadda about it, Gramps? You got a tackle box in your rig?" Ike said to the hunter. He was standing kind of bent over from the stinging in his rear.

The old man seemed happy to have something to do and opened the trunk of his Ford. Sure enough, he pulled out an old dented tackle box and set it on the fender. After a quick rummage around he found some rusty tweezers. Ike didn't look all that enthused about having those messing around in his rear end.

"Well, if that's all ya got, that's all ya got," he mumbled.

Under normal circumstances those rusty tweezers would have looked deadly, but thinking about Ike getting tetanus in his butt sort of inspired me a little. No doubt it hurt, tetanus that is. Otherwise, no one would make such a fuss over stepping on a silly rusty nail.

Gram said that it was the blood poisoning that would kill ya, and I knew that those rusty tweezers could be Ike's ticket to a good case of blood poisoning, not a bad idea considering all the mischief Ike'd been up to in his life. Remembering it was me who was doing the poking sort of flattened out the fun, though.

Ike saw the whiskey sitting on the ground and grabbed up the bottle and took a huge snort. That's when Dreggs realized we'd taken his booze.

"You stole my whiskey? Why you little weasels!" For a second I thought Dreggs might do something rash and make it impossible to work on Ike.

"Easy there, Dreggs! Let the kid get me unpeppered first. Then you can kill 'em."

Dreggs calmed down and grabbed the bottle and sucked on it like a thirsty baby.

"We'll need some of that whiskey to dunk those rusty tweezers," the old hunter said. That instantly spoiled my "giving Ike tetanus" idea. I was planning on not washing them and just making a show of it. Ike heard him, though, and grabbed the tweezers and poured whiskey all over them.

"Okay, where'd ya want me?"

"Across the back of the pickup," the old hunter offered. "I've done a little doctorin' in my time. I can give a hand."

Ike looked him over and then waddled back to the tailgate of the pickup. He pulled up his shirt and there were five or six little pink holes with crusty blood around them. I bit my cheek to give myself a jolt. Not passing out right about now, I felt, was pretty important. Ike laid down on the tailgate. Suddenly, having Ike in the operating room had everyone's attention, and Dreggs didn't notice James saunter over behind us. Everyone was watching closely as I slid those nasty, fishy tweezers inside a puffy hole. Ike instantly stiffened, but didn't yelp or nothing. The thing I realized was I didn't really need my eyes and closed them so I didn't have to watch. I wormed my way in further and then felt something hard.

"You got one?" asked the hunter.

"I think so," I whispered.

"Those are skinny tweezers, so you gotta kind of push it along the side and pop it out. You can't really grab 'em like you could with real doctor's tweezers."

I followed his direction and, sure enough, the little pellet popped out and slithered down Ike's back, leaving a gooey trail.

Dreggs guffawed and relaxed against the side of the truck. Just like that, the first one was finished.

"Ya did it, Cal," James cheered.

"Gimme that whiskey," Ike demanded.

Dreggs handed him the bottle and Ike took another huge snort.

Once I got the hang of it, it didn't take me long to dig the rest of the pellets out of Ike's back. After some more whiskey, Ike wasn't feeling much pain and dropped his pants without a second thought. He flopped over the tailgate of the truck, and me and the old hunter looked at each other. I must have had a pretty sour look because Dreggs burst out laughing and pointed at our shocked faces.

"They're not likin' yer smile, there Ikeiii," he snickered. I again looked at the hunter and winced. He nodded toward Ike's pink rump and I gingerly slipped the tweezers into the first red hole.

"I gotta go see a man about a horse," Dreggs announced. He'd finished off the whiskey and weaved off into the woods.

Out of the corner of my eye I detected the hunter signaling to James. I looked at James and he was nodding his head. He slithered off and over to the Ford and grabbed a box of 30-30 shells out of the trunk. I had the tweezers inside Ike's flesh and just moved them around while cautiously watching James. He noticed something else and grabbed a tire iron and quietly came back. He slipped the iron to the hunter who held it tight.

For as long as James and me have been defying natural law and staying alive, something always would pop up—a branch to grab while sliding down some hill, enough gas to get a fire going when we were freezing in the snow, a hole to wiggle out of some mine shaft. It was always something, which is why I wasn't all that surprised when the hunter bonked Ike on the head and slid him off to the side.

"Get in the back," the hunter hissed at us. We hurried and jumped into the bed of the truck. He didn't slam the door until he had it started and jammed into gear.

That's when Dreggs popped out of the woods and leveled the shotgun right at James and me. We ducked, but nothing happened.

"He didn't reload!" I whispered. "It's a single shot and he didn't reload!"

The hunter wheeled that truck around and I thought for sure it would come apart. It held together, though, and we bounced down the road. I saw Dreggs trying to stuff Ike into the Ford as we peeled off.

Great, now we get to be a part of a chase scene, I thought. I loved chase scenes in the movies. Especially when the cars went up on two wheels with the cops hanging out the windows shooting like crazy. I'd forget to blink until it was over and sometimes they'd last a while and my eyes got dry. But, suddenly, becoming the guys being chased didn't look so fun. I grabbed the tailgate and we got it up and latched.

"If they start shootin' at us," I hollered, "stay below the tailgate!"

James just nodded. It had all happened so fast we were both still reeling from the thought that we'd escaped.

The Ford didn't appear and we hit each other on the shoulder, our way of saying we made it.

The old hunter never slowed and we were holding on as he skidded and bounced that old Chevy down the mountain road. Just as fast as we got excited, our hope suddenly drained away when the Ford came tearing around a corner in hot pursuit. I looked at James.

"Ya know, Dreggs has to kill us, don't ya?" he stated. I just nodded. He looked around at the hunter.

"This old clunker's never gonna outrun that Ford," James shouted. "I hope this old guy's a creative driver."

Creative drivers is what James likes to call the gangsters in the movies who did tricky stuff with their cars.

"Me too," I agreed.

We hunkered down, but kept peeking over the tailgate, watching Dreggs eat up the road between us.

It didn't take long for him to be right behind us and start ramming that Ford into our truck. That smashing tossed James and me around like beach balls. All we could do was grab the sides and hold on.

The hunter had that old truck's gas to the floor, but it just didn't have the beans to outrun that V8 Ford. What was making our ride even more fun was the hunter weaving back and forth trying to dodge Dreggs' ramming.

We were staying low, but I snuck a peek over the side and my eyes about popped out of my head.

"We're going into the canyon," I shouted.

James had to also sneak a peek. His eyes said the same thing, "DANG!"

The Salmon River canyon was a deep cut through the mountains that divided Mud Lake from Stevensville. On our right was nothing but a steep two hundred foot drop into the treacherous river.

The old hunter obviously knew the risk and tried to keep the truck as far from the right side of the gravel road as possible. It was the blind curves, though, that always forced him back on the right side and that's when Dreggs would make his moves.

The first time Dreggs came alongside, James and me could see his evil face glancing over at the truck and then he started slamming into us. The truck swerved wildly to the left and gravel spit out into empty space.

We exchanged a look of terror. This was it. We'd run out of rope and still had space to drop!

The old guy was some kind of driver, though. He managed to get the truck back on the road and slammed into the Ford. Dreggs hadn't expected that and skipped off the rock face that shouldered the other side of the narrow mountain road. But he got the Ford pointed back at us, and continued ramming the old Chevy truck from behind. In a way, this was better because he couldn't get around to the side and work us off that cliff. The hunter knew this, too, and did his best to keep Dreggs behind and off our side. But, it was those dang curves—not knowing if someone was coming—that kept pushing us back to the left. And then, there it was!

A car suddenly appeared around the blind corner and Dreggs nearly smashed into it head on.

The driver must have had a heart attack when he saw the Ford coming right at him! Dreggs slammed on his brakes in the nick of time and swerved back behind us.

By now, James and me decided we'd better start watching, just in case we needed to jump or something. That's when I got the idea to help out.

"Hey, let's grab that tire and toss it out," I shouted. I'd suddenly realized there was stuff in the back of this old farm truck and we wrestled the spare tire into position.

Dreggs was hanging back, probably catching his breath after his near hit. That's when we pitched that tire out the back. It took a wild bounce and landed right on the windshield of the Ford. Dreggs swerved wildly, but regained control of the car. Our spirits jumped and then crashed almost at the same time. We started rooting around for other stuff and found some engine parts, which we pitched at the Ford. Except, Dreggs dropped back out of range. That gave him time to swerve around the debris we were using as bombs.

We tried everything. The off-set dump to try and catch him on a swerve and pop his tires. The fast ball with four-inch bolts that were banging around in the truck bed. The high throw, which generally missed due to his swerving. Before long we were out of ammunition and pitching styles and slumped back and held on.

"Looks like Ike's awake."

Sure enough, Ike slumped over the seat and seemed surprised to be in the car with Dreggs, who popped him one in the head. Ike then slugged Dreggs in the shoulder. Their Ford swerved like crazy. We could see both criminals' eyes look like saucers. Ike must have realized him smacking Dreggs during the car chase put them in danger and climbed over the seat.

We were in the middle of a skinny old bridge when Dreggs made another move to our side. But, an old lady was coming the other way and just about slammed into Dreggs. He swerved and nicked her bumper and spun out as she skidded against the rail and stopped.

As we sped off the bridge, I looked down and could just make out the Salmon River at the bottom of the canyon.

"That's way down there," I muttered to myself.

The old hunter got a lead on Dreggs, but not for long. Dreggs soon caught back up and that's when he made his move. He jammed the car forward and came alongside again. Ike pointed the 410 shotgun out the window and made like he was going to shoot, but we both knew he didn't have any shells and ignored him. It was the slamming into the side of the truck that had us worried.

Our driver again had to allow enough room on a blind curve, which Dreggs grabbed.

SLAM! WHAM! Dreggs was really pouring it on. He hit the truck and just locked on, pushing us over. The truck's tires started to shriek as the hunter turned into Dreggs and the two rigs locked together. Suddenly, one of our tires exploded with a loud POP and the truck veered wildly to the left.

We hit the edge and skidded along the gravel shoulder for fifty yards and then, like in the movies, we started to roll?. . . in slow motion. That's when James and me were both flung out of the bed like toy dolls.

I landed in a large clump of maples while James lit in a shale slide, and started to slide and tumble toward the bottom of the canyon. Not far from him was the old truck, smashing into parts and pieces.

James skidded into a bunch of limbs in the middle of the shale and stopped. He just lay there looking pretty wrung out, while the truck finally hit a fir tree and jammed to a stop. The hunter was still inside the cab, looking lifeless.

After watching James and the Chevy truck catapult down the hill, I laid still for a few moments just taking stock of everything. Then, I felt a terrible urge to get to James and see if he was alive.

As I moved, everything hurt plenty, but it didn't feel like I'd broken anything, which was a miracle and a huge relief.

I'd busted both my arms and my leg once and knew what that felt like. I realized I wasn't hurt that bad, not like James and the old hunter probably were. I was going to be sore, though.

James wasn't moving, and neither was the hunter.

◇ **CHAPTER 10** ◇

Death in the Canyon

I heard the Ford skid to a stop up on the road and decided I needed to get moving. I was the closest one to the top, so I untangled myself from the maples and started working my way down into the canyon. It wasn't that hard—gravity was on my side and the shale rock helped me slide. There were plenty of limbs and young whippy trees to grab and I made it to James just as Dreggs came to the edge of the road.

I got down behind James, who wasn't moving, and laid still myself. Dreggs was looking down trying to see if we were alive or not, so he'd know if he had to come down and finish us off.

There wasn't any movement in the truck, which I figured made Dreggs happy.

"Don't move, James," I whispered. "Dreggs is up there, but he might think were done in if we hold still."

It was a stupid suggestion because James looked

pretty banged up. Moving wasn't really on his mind.

I sneaked a peek uphill and Dreggs had disappeared. I waited to hear the car start.

"Maybe you should try to get to the truck and see how the hunter's doin'," James moaned.

"We need to wait here for a bit. I don't think they've left yet," I whispered and positioned myself so I could see the road. I watched as Dreggs and Ike appeared. I couldn't hear what they were saying, but they started dragging their feet over the area where we'd skidded off.

"They're trying to hide where we went off," I whispered.

"Are they looking like they're gonna come down?" James asked. It took some effort for James to talk, let alone think.

"I dunno. If they do, they'll have people stopping to see what's up. I don't think they're gonna want to do any explaining."

"You just keep thinkin' like that. You'll have us home in no time. It's do or die time, Cal." Coming from James, the undisputed leader of our adventures, that was a supreme compliment.

It seemed like a long time until Dreggs and Ike felt they'd disguised our skid marks and I heard the car start.

"Looks like we're going to just die down here." My voice actually sounded cheerful. Dying slow down here in the canyon actually sounded better than Dreggs or Ike beating in our brains. At least we had some hope in this canyon.

The Ford spit gravel as Dreggs and Ike left the scene.

"Okay, they're gone," I said. "We gotta get either up or down. What do you think's best?" I didn't feel much like climbing up that steep wall, but going down didn't sound all that fun either. I really wanted to know James' thoughts.

"You're the brains of this operation," he said slow and slurred and punctuated with a slight bloody grin. He grabbed my arm. "Up. We can get a ride home." He tried to move, but his body hurt in a hundred places.

Something struck me. I shook my head, no.

"What if those two gangsters are laying up somewhere and then just come strolling back, hoping to nab us when we've climbed outta here?"

James nodded a little. He agreed. "It's gotta be eatin' at ol' Dreggs that we'd seen Jenkins."

"Yeah," I agreed, deciding not to again rub in the fact that James had spilled those beans. "Down then, I like gravity today."

I glanced up to make sure one of them hadn't hung back to see how we really were. No one stood there watching. I gently lifted James' arm and helped him sit.

"Ohhhh, man. This is worse than the time in the mine shaft."

That had been a bad day. James fell while showing off inside the beam structure of the mine and got caught hanging upside down with this leg jammed and twisted. It didn't break, but his knee was pretty touchy for a while. I had to lift him up and hold him while he untangled his screaming leg, and then help him back to daylight.

This was much worse.

Being all banged up, it wasn't easy getting down to the Chevy truck. James especially had a hard time not sliding down the hillside and I couldn't stop worrying that Dreggs and Ike were going to pop their heads over the edge and start shooting.

When we reached the truck, we saw that the hunter was in really bad condition. He was alive, but busted in a lot of important places.

"Mister, I'm gonna go get some help," I explained.

He opened his eyes a little.

"Name's Al . . . Alfred . . . Alfred Leland," he croaked out. Talking took wind that he couldn't really spare.

"Mister Al, we're not sure what to do, but it looks like those two thugs took off. So, we got some time." I tried to sound reassuring.

"But, we're thinking we should go down, not up . . . if they're waiting up there for us."

He kind of nodded his head. "What's got them so hot after you two?"

"We found a guy they'd killed. And then, they figured out that we knew about it." I decided to not mention that James was the one who let that cat outta the bag.

"Ummm," he acknowledged. "There's a chance they'll be gunnin' for ya, all right." He coughed and sputtered blood all over his tee shirt. "I'm not sure where I stand, though. You two best get going and try to get some help."

James had wedged himself to keep from sliding down the hill. His eyes were closed, obviously hurting a lot. He rolled his head to look at me.

"You go, Cal. I'll stay here," James muttered.

His suggestion seemed the right thing to do. I just couldn't get my mind around me going down the river by myself, without James' help. I hardly ever did stuff by myself. Stuff like this, I mean. The most adventure I ever undertook by myself was to go fishing up near the mill. And that was always in broad daylight. The way the sun was hanging low on the canyon wall clued me in that it wouldn't be light for much longer.

I'd never go into a mine or old cabin without James. What fun would that be?

"But . . .," I stopped. But what? But something! "But, I can't go down the river by myself, James."

"And I can't go down with you, dork. Look at me. There's no way I could make it down that canyon," he moaned. "I'll stay here and keep us alive until you get back with some help." He motioned toward Mr. Leland.

James was right and I knew it.

"You can do it, Cal." James was looking at me in a way I'd never seen before. He meant it. He meant to shove me off into the abyss of my own abilities and decisions . . . decisions that could make the difference between all of us surviving.

"Son, listen," Alfred sputtered, looking over at James. "I don't think I'm gonna make it, here. I'm thinkin' you should just head on down the Salmon with him. You boys get yerselves helped. If'n I make it . . . I make it. If not, well, you sittin' here bleedin' out too won't help any."

"Mr. Leland, Cal knows how to do this, and he can do it a lot faster without draggin' me along." James was respectful, but firm that I should go alone. "Cal, that's it. You can move a lot faster without me."

"OKAY!" I snapped, too loud. "I will! But before I go, I'm gonna get you some water and we gotta get Mr. Leland outta that truck."

The old guy resigned himself to James staying and let out a sigh and a sputter. He looked at me. It took just about all he had to talk anymore.

"Young man, that bridge we crossed a ways back, that's High Bridge. Once you get down into the canyon, it's shorter back up to the bridge than anything you'll find downstream. It'll be a climb outta there, but you can catch a ride."

James looked at me and agreed that was a good idea.

It only took me about thirty minutes to fill a coffee can we'd found in the truck cab with water and claw myself back to the truck. Then it took all of our strength and grit to peel Mr. Leland from the mangled old Chevy truck and get him sort of comfortable. He couldn't really lie flat because his chest was pretty banged up. But, James and me tore up our clothes and made bandages for all of us and I decided to make one more run for water and then started off.

The sun had crawled out of the canyon by then and it was starting to get chilly. I was glad I'd taken a few more minutes to tear off some fir bows to cover Mr. Leland. While I was doing that, James and me tried to thank him for saving us.

He just sort of chuckled and said, "Outta the fryin' pan, into the fire." I'd heard that phrase before, and I'd had fresh trout flip out of the frying pan and land in our campfire. He meant that our troubles hadn't gone away . . . just changed.

* * *

When I hit the bottom of the canyon it was rough going from the start, climbing over the huge boulders and mossy spots. I wasn't expecting anything else. Gramps and me had hiked into the Salmon River canyon a couple of times right after I'd moved here, and I remember having to carefully pick my footing because of the wet moss. He wouldn't let me come down by myself . . . not that I would. Like I said, I pretty much played it safe unless James or Gramps was around.

I loved the fishing down here, but hated the slippery rocks inside the deep, narrow canyon. The spray from the boiling river kept everything more or less soaked year round and the rocks were like snot. It had seemed to take forever to get anywhere back when Gramps and I had come down here, and it wasn't any different now.

My Keds still didn't want to grip anything. Those TV commercials for Keds . . . they lied.

It was after about the fifth fall and banged shin that I decided to just tramp right up the middle. By then my feet and legs were wet and I'd more or less gotten used to the freezing water.

Even though the spring runoff was months past, the glacier-cold water still made a person think twice before jumping in. The trouble was, if I was going to make any time at all, I had to bite the bullet and go right up the middle whenever I could.

The Salmon River had carved what is more or less a channel through the mountains. During the spring, this river raged high and white, continuing to cut and chisel its way to the center of the earth. Fishing was impossible until maybe August, and then you had to know where to go.

Gramps told me there are places that are at least ten feet deeper today than when he was a kid. He showed me a spot where he and his buddies used to sit and fish. That ledge was eight feet above the highest waterline.

So, for James to poke me in the butt and tell me to hustle on upriver and get some help was no small thing. Anything looking like "hustle" took me straight up the middle, or as close to the middle as I could go.

The cold, my empty stomach, my own bruises and scrapes from the roll off the hill, were like dragging a sack of sand with me. I had to stop and rest pretty often, most times next to some slack water that eddied out into large pools.

I wished like crazy I'd had a spinner on a line. I would have loved to drop it in that deep green water and munch a sandwich and sip on a Coke.

"There's fish down there, for sure," I muttered as I unfolded my stiff legs and worked myself around one pool that looked particularly inviting.

Gramps taught me to fish. Long before I actually moved up to live with them he'd get me off somewhere and we'd sit and reel in the fish. I didn't really care what kind of fishing we did. Just so long as there was sandwiches and Nehi's or Cokes involved, and Gramps. He was tons of fun and we'd laugh and compete on who could catch the most or biggest fish. That was before he got sick. After that, he didn't want to go much at all, and Dad didn't like fishing and neither did James. So, my fishing just became the easy Mill Pond or Mud Lake. I'd try to get Dad to take me when he came up to visit, after I'd moved up with Gramps and Gram, and he'd fake like he was enjoying himself. The trouble is, I know what liking fishing looks like and Dad didn't have the look. He'd just stick his pole in the seat or a rock and read a book or gripe about his crappy boss or something. I quit asking him to take me and he didn't seem to mind that I quit asking.

Gramps, though, that first summer, took me all the time. Mud Lake, Mosquito Lake, Salmon River canyon.

"Even the larger irrigation ditches have fighters hidin' out," he said once when we'd stopped to check some sprinkler pipes.

He showed me how to let my line drift under the bridge, and sure enough, a little popper grabbed my worm and took off running.

I'd been thinking pretty hard about Gramps and fishing, and James, and how we'd gotten into this mess when High Bridge came into view . . . sort of.

* * *

I have no idea how long I'd splashed and wormed

my way through the narrow spaces and over boulders, but it was well dark when I made out the shape of the bridge.

I'd heard of High Bridge and knew that there was a trail that led down to the water. For a long time fishermen had slithered down through the trees and rocks to nab the very fish I'd been dreaming of; the ones lurking on the bottoms of all those pools and eddies I'd splashed through.

If there really was a trail it would be hard to see and I had no idea which side of the river it was on. Fishermen were well known for just diving off into the wild brush, caught in a fever of trout madness. Who cared how to get back up the steep sides. I'd even suffered from a kid's version of the sickness and stole the mill boat one time. I didn't care that it wasn't mine, or that they'd pulled the drain plug against kids just like me. By the time I got it rowed back, I had three lake trout and a half sunk boat.

I scanned the side of the river I was on and found a spot that looked scuffed and tramped down a bit. As I started pulling myself up, using limbs and saplings as handholds, it was pretty obvious that this was the little path. I made it about half way up before needing to rest, which is when I heard voices . . . low men's voices.

Because of the trees, it was hard to see the bridge, but suddenly the glow from a cigarette caught my eye and I tried like mad to focus.

It struck me that I had been pretty quiet while climbing up, that whoever that was hadn't heard me. Of course, my sounds were mixed in with the frothy roar of the river. It made me feel kind of proud. James and me always tried to be as invisible as possible. We never knew when we'd have to lay low and let some danger pass or go unseen for a while. Laying low for a few minutes is exactly what I decided to do.

Since yesterday, I had gained a new appreciation for animals that didn't just barge right out there and get themselves killed. After a few minutes, I started to work my way further up the mountainside, taking even more care not to slip or crack a limb or something.

From time to time, I could still see the cigarette glow and hear talking. Whoever that was wasn't too worried about being heard. They weren't yelling or anything. They just weren't being watchful like I was. I started to wonder if maybe it could be Dreggs and Ike.

Mr. Leland's words popped into my mind: "There's a chance they'll be gunnin' for ya, all right."

I was stuck, at least until daylight, when I could see who it was. By then, though, Mr. Leland could be dead, and maybe James too.

I was still thinking about them lying there, probably cold, when I heard a car coming along up on the gravel road. I had a sudden desire to make a run up the hill and try to wave it down. Before I could move, it rounded the bend and flashed its lights across the bridge. What stopped me cold was . . . there wasn't anyone there! Just a few seconds before the car had come, I'd heard them talking, and now there wasn't anyone. That got the hair standing up on the back of my neck. Now, I was going to be careful. Why had they ducked out of sight?

Maybe it really was Dreggs and Ike.

I held still and waited. Pretty soon, the voices started again. Then, a match sparked and lit up a man's face? . . . a skinny face with beady eyes. Ike! Standing there by himself.

My heart sank. Mr. Leland had been right, and I was too. Those two murderers knowing we knew about old Jenkins, well, they just weren't going to let that get out.

As I peeked out through the trees, I could see him milling around. Then, Ike started talking to himself in the dark. I could see the red point of the cigarette waving around, kind of like Uncle Neal's did when he used to drive home a point with Gramps. He'd wave his hand in the air and I'd sit and just watch that red glow make lines in the dark on Gram's porch.

Man, that guy just gets creepier and creepier, I thought, as I watched Ike's cigarette cherry wave around in the dark. Now that I knew who it was, I could make out his voice better, and it struck me that it had been Ike talking to himself the whole time.

He was working on some plan to get the money and get rid of Dreggs. I could only catch bits and pieces, but there was money involved and Dreggs' fat . . . which had to go.

One good thing about that car passing was it showed me I was almost level with the bridge. For what good that did me, I didn't know yet.

If Ike's here alone, where's Dreggs? A wave of panic washed over me.

"They must have divided up," I whispered to myself. "Oh great, now I'm talking to myself!" I continued, still talking softly to myself.

Where's the Ford? I ran back through my mind that the curves in the road had been very narrow. Would there be a place to park?

Would Dreggs want someone to see the Ford and recognize it? Especially with it now completely beat up from bashing us.

My mind was in high gear wondering if Dreggs had gone back to try and finish off James and me and Alfred. I decided I needed to hear my voice to try and untangle my thoughts and started to whisper very low.

"There's not gonna be any place to park the Ford back on that curve."

As if James was sitting right next to me, and we were working on a plan together, I heard his voice in my head. "So, then the Ford's here. I'll bet Ike's supposed to go back and pick up Dreggs."

"Why's Ike standing around here? Why aren't they getting on down the road?" I whispered.

"They're not takin' any chances," I heard James' voice explain inside my head.

"You mean Ike's waiting to see if we come along the river? Why would Dreggs leave Ike alone? He probably suspects that Ike tried to ditch him," I muttered very low.

"Dreggs must've kept somethin' Ike wants. That's why he's standin' out there figurin'," the James voice reasoned.

"Yeah," I agreed. "Otherwise, Ike'd just leave."

"That's why he's peeved off and arguing about it," the James voice answered.

I almost crowed. "Now we're figuring this out!" I caught myself almost saying it too loud.

So, wadda we do? I thought. I decided talking out loud was dangerous. I gotta see if the Ford's here.

It didn't take me long to find the road and stay quiet while doing it. It was so dark, I literally had to feel my way along, so when I got to the road it was a surprise. The gravel crunched under foot and I instantly withdrew back a step. I strained my eyes to see if Ike had heard me. I hadn't seen the glow of his smoke for a while and stood stone still, waiting.

"You think you got it figured out?" Ike snarled to himself. "I'm the one who's got it figured."

A tiny red bean appeared as Ike sucked on his smoke. He blew out hard and went on yapping to himself.

"I'd a never chose Yuma, ya fat pig. Southern Cal's what I'd do. More people. We can blend in. Slip across at night and we're home free," he laughed to himself. "Ouch! Damnit!"

He must have bumped his back side on something. I smiled, thinking of those pellets still in his butt.

"Fester baby, fester!" I muttered, meaning it.

"I'll give ya Mexico," Ike growled to himself. "I won't give ya how we get there. Or when! We need to stop messing around with these kids and get going."

Ike tossed the cigarette over the side of the bridge and started walking toward me. I could hear the crunching of his shoes on the gravel.

I was tucked in pretty good. All I had to do was stop living when he passed. It was the thundering in my chest that had me worried.

Fortunately, the rumble of the Salmon River drifted up and helped mask the other night noises, including the bass drum in my ears. I did hear the jingle of car keys, however, just after I started to breathe again and Ike was twenty feet past me . . . and then the Ford's door opened? . . . painfully, but it didn't close. A sudden flash of a match flame lit another one of Ike's cigarettes. I saw that he was seated in the Ford with his legs kicked out in the gravel.

So, the Ford was here! Now, how to get it away from Ike, get help, all before Dreggs finishes off James and Mr. Leland!

The pressure was pounding in my head, and I started to breathe fast and clamped my hand over my mouth to quiet the wheezing sound that had suddenly started.

I gotta create a diversion. But, how? That's when that nervous little weasel, Ike, got up and started walking around again, in the general direction of where I had been wheezing. Not as though he heard the sound . . . nope, he was too busy talking out loud to himself. As he got closer, I started moving backwards toward the rear of the Ford.

I had a sickening feeling we were about to become reacquainted.

◇ CHAPTER 11 ◇

Outsmarting Thugs Ain't Easy

The fact that no one hardly ever drove this road left it up to me to come up with something, and quick. If Ike took off, there I'd be, sitting alone with no plan.

Ike walked past where I'd just been hiding. I could just make out his silhouette against the black trees and the night sky.

I'd managed to sneak around through the woods to the back of the Ford and was inching closer when he turned and started wandering back. I hunkered down about twenty feet behind the car.

"They ain't comin'," he snorted and tossed his cigarette out. He sat back down in the driver's seat and wrestled with the door to get it closed, but it was pretty scraped up from Dreggs' skip off the rock wall earlier. As he was wrenching it around I was able to slide up a little closer.

Ike turned on the key and started cranking the

engine, which refused to start.

It was flooded, like Mr. Leland said it did sometimes. An idea started to brew and I groped around for a large stick or rock. Ike started cranking again. "Come on you piece a . . ." A loud sputter drowned out his words and then the car sat quiet. "Okay, what's your problem?" Ike complained.

It's flooded, I thought, and tossed a long stick across the road and ducked back down.

The stick hit the trees and shuffled through the limbs to the ground. The soft swishing sound it made as it fell through the trees got Ike's attention.

More than actually see him, I could feel him suddenly go still. He stopped moving and listened. I held my breath and waited.

There was no way to quietly exit the rumpled old Ford. Everything about it creaked and squeaked as Ike decided to go investigate. The thing I listened for the closest was the keys . . . I didn't hear them jingle. That was good, except now it was DO or DIE time?. . . again. It was starting to seem like my whole life had become one long string of DO or DIES. I slowly sucked in a deep breath and peeked around the fender.

Ike was inching across the road, trying so hard not to make any sound, which was impossible in the gravel.

Because of the darkness, I really couldn't see how far he'd gone, but the crunch of his shoes told me he was about as far as he was going to go.

"Okay, you two," he ordered to the dark. "The jig's up. You come on out and I won't hurt ya." He stood and listened for a second.

"I'm plannin' on ditchin' Ol' Dreggs as soon as I can, and I'll get you two outta here too."

His feet crunched a little more and I stood up and tossed another stick, just a little past where he stood. I heard Ike's feet freeze and then move toward the sound. I made my move.

I slunk around the car and jumped into the driver's seat, but didn't try to close the door. I cranked the key with my foot jamming the gas to the floor and the old run-out Ford coughed to life!

It was already in gear when I popped the clutch and the car literally leaped forward. The gas was pushed so hard to the floor that the tires spit gravel for probably twenty yards.

Ike grabbed for the door, but didn't make it. He was able to jump onto the rear trunk, though, as I peeled out!

I looked in the rear view mirror and there he was, smashed against the glass, clinging for life! I didn't know what to do about him, so I just sped off across the bridge and went around the corner in a slide. My plan hadn't included a passenger and so I had to keep my speed up to not give Ike an opportunity to climb in. It didn't take much imagination to figure what that would be like if Ike got inside.

"Hey, come on! I won't hurt ya! I mean it! Just stop!" He seemed to mouth through the glass.

"Yeah, right," I muttered. "Not a chance, killer."

Once moving, I pulled hard on the door and finally got it to latch, kind of. It gave me some relief that I wouldn't fly out on a sharp corner.

The road was such a curvy little one-and-a-half laner that it took all I had to keep the car from sliding off the edge. I hadn't wanted to drive this fast, but I felt if I slowed at all, Ike could get a foothold and work his way around.

As best I could in the dark, I kept one eye on him, watching for any change. If it looked like he was getting comfortable, I'd give the wheel a jerk and he'd paste himself back against the steel and glass.

I could actually hear him now. "Ahhh! You're gonna

kill me!" He was really scared.

"How's it feel," I shouted back.

The last thing I wanted on my conscience was another dead guy. I hadn't really been able to get the old wino who fell off the train out of my mind, but I knew something had to be done about Ike before too long.

He hates you, Cal. He was probably going to kill you and James. He ran you off the road and over the side of the mountain. I was reciting to myself as I careened down the mountain road. If you get there and Dreggs is there, then you got both of them to deal with.

I gritted my teeth and looked for a rock wall which wasn't hard to find. Much of the road had been blasted out of sheer rock. I checked on Ike and saw that he was climbing up the back and onto the top of the car. All I could see were his feet.

Suddenly, his arm reached in the driver window and was grabbing for me! I was now trying to drive and swat his hand out of my face. I instinctively started rolling up the window and caught his arm.

"Ahhhh! Open the window, boy!"

"Forget it," I screamed back, his hand and forearm still lashing wildly around in my face.

A straight cut wall approached on the right and I drove right alongside and then jammed the wheel to the right and the car glanced off with a loud scrapping sound.

What happened next is kind of hard to tell. I'm not used to seeing someone twist around and flipping and flopping like a Raggedy Andy Doll in a storm.

Ike slid off the car and was hanging by his arm as I sped down the gravel road. He was twisted backwards while his free arm flailed wildly, trying to find anything to grab. His screams and curses were like something from one of my scary headhunter dreams . . . you know, the kind where someone's being boiled or something. Really horrible, and I can't really get his hollering out of my mind even today.

His hand that was locked inside with me was grabbing at everything it could find. It found my shirt and locked on. His fingers dug into my shoulder and I sped up. His yelling got louder and more terrified. At the same time, his outside hand was tearing at the paint, the tiny rain gutters, trying to reach inside the window. Then it found the handle.

The pain in my shoulder was getting worse and for some reason I did the best thing I could . . . I did it without even really thinking. I rolled down the window and Ike's arm was sucked out like it had gone up a vacuum cleaner hose!

I instantly looked in the mirror and saw him, in the pale night-light, tumble and roll and come to a stop in a tangled ball and lay still.

I skidded to a stop and looked out the window; I could hardly believe what had just happened. As if flying off a cliff in an old pickup wasn't enough, I'd just dragged Ike a couple hundred yards at forty miles an hour. Now he was back there looking like a giant mangled pretzel.

"Nobody's gonna believe this, when I tell 'em," I mumbled.

The ball of twisted legs and arms that was Ike suddenly moved and started to unwrap himself. He tried to get up, but only managed to sit there. He saw me and lifted his arm in a kind of wave. Then he painfully motioned for me to come help him.

What a kook, I thought. When he began to crawl toward the car, I didn't wait around to see anymore. I jammed the Ford into gear and lurched off around the next bend and back up to speed.

I didn't stop again for about half a mile. I needed to catch my breath. I felt dizzy. Maybe I was going to have a seizure after all. If I did, it would be from hunger and exhaustion.

A thin moon had come up and I could see a little of the road and I looked around. It dawned on me that there was no way I'd know where the truck had driven off the cliff, so how could I even try and help James and Mr. Leland.

We'd been the ones going off the cliff and hadn't really been paying close attention to the surroundings. A big tree. I remembered seeing a big tree as I flew through the air.

Okay, a big tree in a land of big trees. A bend in a road with a thousand bends. It all looked the same. Even standing here, this bend looked just like the last bend.

I didn't know what to do. I figured this road went down the hill to Stevensville.

But how far? And I didn't know the turns or what roads went where. If it was anything like Mud Lake, the locals would have messed up the signs just to get people lost. And, there was still Dreggs. What was he up to? Thinking of Dreggs caused me to suddenly climb back into the car and lock all the doors, driving ahead slowly.

$$\diamond \textbf{ CHAPTER 12 } \diamond$$

Lock the Doors and Don't Panic

Once locked inside the Ford, I felt a little safer, and crept along at about fifteen miles per hour. I'd thought it through that if Dreggs was waiting for Ike where we crashed, he'd see the car coming and step out to catch Ike's attention. And that Ike would probably be driving along at a slow speed, not knowing exactly where Dreggs would be. Still, fifteen was fast enough for me to get away if he tried to jump the car or something. I was pretty nervous. That Dreggs was a slippery devil and he might have something planned just in case Ike blew it, which of course he had.

While I was wondering about all the what-ifs, the only good headlight caught a small piece of rag jammed into the rocks.

"That's it, I bet," I whispered.

I went past about two hundred yards and found a place to turn around. I was very careful to watch all around me in case Dreggs popped out of nowhere. The Ford's headlight showed me that there wasn't anyone up ahead, and so I went back.

I did this a couple of times, back and forth, just to make sure. On my third pass by the rag I saw where the truck had skidded off the road. I pulled over to the edge and stopped and waited. I inched down the window a little and looked all around me again. It sure seemed like the coast was clear. I squeezed my lips up to the little sliver of open window and hollered.

"James!"

"Yeah! Cal?"

"Yeah. It's me! How are ya?"

"We're alive, but freezin' cold."

The sound of James' voice sounded so good. I reached for the door handle. But stopped. The question of Dreggs was still unanswered and I started to get nervous. He could be just hanging back, waiting for me to show up.

"Have you seen Dreggs?" It was all I could do to shout out his name, thinking he'd pop out . . .

"Here I am, ya little puke!"

"He's down in the canyon," James yelled. "Broken leg, I think. He's been hollerin' at me all night."

"This ain't over, punk!" Dreggs' voice echoed up from the dark.

I couldn't believe my ears. I pushed open the door and got close to the edge.

"What about Ike?" James asked.

"Ike was waitin' at the bridge. I stole the Ford."

"Whoa! Cal!" James said, impressed. "Al says to just follow this road down and you'll come to a farm house. Just stay on the main road."

"Okay! Okay! Sit tight!" I yelled back, excited but worried about the criminals who seemed to rise from the grave . . . or at least from the gravel.

◇ **CHAPTER 13** ◇

The Final Shootout

That old Ford started to come apart at the seams banging down that mountain road. Truth is, I pushed it farther than I should and way more than my skimpy driving experience. I was so excited to have Dreggs and Ike off our trail that I wished that old car had wings.

I passed the farm before I realized it was there and skidded to a stop. A light came on upstairs when I started pounding on the horn while tearing down the driveway; and when I skidded up to the porch, the skinniest man I'd ever seen was standing there stringing on his coveralls with a shotgun in his hands.

He didn't seem all that excited to see a kid explode out of Mr. Leland's Ford either.

"What's all the fuss, young feller?" he said, squinting into the dark car. "You got Alfred in there with ya?"

I rushed around the backside of the car.

"Mister, Mister Leland and my pal, James, are stuck

in the . . ."

THUD! I landed on the ground like a sack as my shirt caught on a piece of twisted metal on the Ford and yanked me backwards.

He hurried over and poked his head around the fender at me lying with my arm up in the air.

"You okay, young man?"

"Yeah, we got to get back up the canyon before Dreggs gets to 'em!"

"Dreggs? Who's Dreggs?"

The old duffer was starting to make me worry that I'd found the wrong farm. He just wasn't in any hurry about anything.

"Mister, we crashed the truck and Dreggs and Ike stole Mr. Leland's Ford," I tried to explain as I crawled to my feet and gestured to the mangled car. "And they're stuck in the canyon and I dunno where Dreggs is, exactly!" I was breathing like a mad man, probably sounding like one too.

My excitement and a few more details finally got his motor started and he quickly finished buttoning his overalls.

"All right then. You stay right here and Ma and Jenny'll take care of you."

"Wait, you don't even know where to go! We need to call the police and get them up there too!" There was no way I was gonna stick around here and not see what happened.

"Okay, okay, you're right there, young man."

Just then, Ma and Jenny appeared at the door, both looking sleepy.

"What's up, Pa?"

"There's been an accident up the canyon and me and this boy here are gonna go see what we can do. Get me some blankets and such and I'll get the truck around."

Ma and Jenny turned to go.

"Oh, call the sheriff and let him know we're on our way," he said.

Ma and Jenny disappeared, and I just stood there by myself. Tiredness suddenly swept over me like a blanket and I flopped down on the porch steps. The thought of calling Gram and letting her know that I was all right nibbled at the corners of my mind. However, I wasn't going to just barge into their house and hunt around for the phone. I knew that if I got Gram on the phone, she'd pretty soon hand it over to Uncle Neal for one of his giant ear whippin's.

I knew that sometimes a good ear whippin' can take some of the fight out of the actual rump whippin' . . . I'd learned to be patient during an ear whippin' so he could use up some of his steam. I just couldn't spare that much time, not with James and Mr. Leland lying out under the stars, freezing cold.

When the farmer's wife came back out with an armful blankets and things, I asked her if she could call my Gram in Mud Lake to let her know I was alright.

"Poag," I said, and then I piled into the truck. The farmer grabbed the shotgun from his wife and put it in the rifle rack and introduced himself as Mr. Murry and we took off.

Once we were driving, I started telling Mr. Murry the story and he started pouring on the gas. He suddenly swerved around a muffler in the road and I smacked my head on the window.

"Dang, someone's been droppin' parts like they left their trunk open."

"That's probably off the Ford, sir. It's pretty banged up from Dreggs rammin' us with it."

Mr. Murry turned and looked at me. "Rammin' ya?"

I jumped ahead to the car chase. He kept flipping his head around at parts of the story, and saying things like: "My-oh-my, son. It's a wonder . . . ." Or, "Goodness, my-oh-my!"

"THERE! See that rag sticking out of the rocks?" I sat up and peered into the dark. The headlights had just glanced off the wall and I saw a flash of white.

Mr. Murry slowed and turned the truck toward the rock wall. There it was, like a little flag, the marker Dreggs had left for Ike. He pulled off to the side and climbed out. For a moment I sat frozen. Ike had suddenly popped into my mind. What about Ike?

"Mr. Murry, that one guy I told you about?. . . Ike? He might just come walkin' along here."

Mr. Murry didn't even hesitate. He reached up to the truck's rifle rack and pulled out his 410 shotgun.

"I hope he does," he said with a stern expression. "Say a prayer, kid. We may need some help."

I jumped out, feeling more confident. I like this prayer stuff. After all, it brought us Mr. Leland and Mr. Murry, didn't it? And got us to James and Mr. Leland.

"JAMES," I yelled into the canyon.

"Cal, you're back!" James' voice echoed off the walls of the canyon. It sounded great.

"I got some help here," I added, excited.

"Alfred? You down there?" Mr. Murry hollered.

"He's doin' okay," James yelled back.

Right then a dusty station wagon rounded the corner, splashing me and Mr. Murry in its headlights. The car skidded to a stop and two burly fellows piled out. They were both about my dad's age and dressed for the cold with flannel shirts and suspenders. Probably hunters.

"What's up, Norm?" one of the men hollered at Mr. Murry.

I was sure glad to hear that they knew Mr. Murry. I wasn't in the mood for more unpredictable people.

"Boy Michael, am I glad to see you. Alfred's run off the road and he and some kid busted up down in the canyon."

"Sure a bunch of hurt people out tonight," Michael said with a puzzled look. "We picked up a guy . . ."

Just then Michael's car revved up and started to roll. That's when I noticed Ike! He'd slid over into the driver's seat and was trying to steal their car!

"HEY," Michael yelled.

Michael and his buddy ran for the car and pulled the door open. Ike was in no shape for a fight and they easily got the car stopped.

"That's the little runt, right there," Ike slurred out through bloody lips. He pointed at me with his good arm. "That's the kid that ran me over in that old Ford and left! Grab 'im!"

Michael and his friend just stood there looking at me, not knowing what to do. Even Mr. Murry was looking at me.

"Boys, I'm not very clear on what all's happened this evening, but I'm pretty sure that's not how it went," Mr. Murry said with an uncertain tone.

"I think we should all just cinch up our britches 'til the sheriff gets here."

I'd told Mr. Murry plenty on the drive up, but I hadn't gotten up to the part about dragging Ike for a couple hundred yards on the gravel road.

I stepped over closer to Mr. Murry. "That's Ike, the one I told you about," I said while watching Ike carefully. "He's the one who killed that hobo." I stepped a little behind Mr. Murry.

"You gonna believe that little rat?" Ike went on. "He's a liar and a car thief! I didn't kill no one!" Ike was trying to get out of the car, but his body was too banged up. All he could do was fall on the ground and flop around like he was made of rubber or something.

"I'm tellin' you suckers that I'm gettin' as far from him as I can! He's one dangerous kid!" Ike started to crawl around the car, trying to give them the slip. Of course, Ike giving those big healthy men the slip would be like a possum trying to sneak past a mountain lion.

"He even kicked me after he ran me over," Ike added for drama.

That's when the hunters started laughing. They grabbed Ike and helped him up, and back into their car. Ike, of course, hollered and complained the whole time.

"You got your guns in there?" I asked. "Better not let him near 'em."

About the time they got Ike simmered down, the sheriff rounded the corner, followed by another pickup, which is also when a loud shot rang out from deep in the canyon.

A piece of rock exploded off the rock wall behind us and everyone scurried for cover.

Ike thought this was a grand new wrinkle and started hollering.

"Yer too high, Dreggs, shoot lower!"

Another report and the wall exploded again.

"I think that's his last round," James yelled up at us.

"Come down here and see, kid!" Dreggs answered back from deep in the canyon. His voice sounded a million miles away.

"That's Dreggs," I whispered to Mr. Murry, who was hunkered down next to me.

By then the sheriff had his gun out and was crouched behind his car, and the guy in the truck had his rifle out too.

"What the heck's goin' on here, Norm?" the sheriff yelled over to us.

"I think we got a couple a wild ones, Sheriff. One of 'em's in Mike's car over there, pretty banged up. And the other's stuck down in the canyon."

"Well, obviously he's still got some fight in him."

"THEY'RE TRYIN' TO GET YA TO . . .," Ike shouted out, but suddenly went quiet when Michael stuffed a rag in his mouth and held it there. "Shhh ummm too goo guuuu" was all that came out after that.

"Keep that guy quiet, Mike," the sheriff commanded.

"I got it, Sheriff," Michael said.

"Okay then, let's see what's going on down there," the sheriff continued. "Carl, I'm gonna set up my light to try and draw his fire. You hurry down the road a ways and see where his shot comes from."

His deputy, Carl, dashed off keeping low, and the sheriff slipped inside his car and flipped on his big spotlight.

We all waited, crouched down behind the cars and trucks, but nothing happened.

"You hold yer fire there, Mister," the sheriff hollered. "You got no chance a gettin' outta there without a fight, ya hear me?"

No more shots pinged off the rocks. As it turned out, Dreggs was out of bullets and pretty willing to let the police drag him up the canyon. His leg was busted and he was badly scraped up from his fall. I guess jail sounded better than lying in the bottom of the canyon.

It seems James had heard Dreggs trying to slither down the loose rock and started throwing rocks at him.

Dreggs got off a few bad shots, but then stumbled when James beaned him with a rock. His tumble over the sharp rocks, and then a hard landing, broke his leg and spanked most of the juice out of him. From then on, James and Alfred were able to rest a little easier. All Dreggs could do was hurl threats and insults up at them. Of course, James took the opportunity to toss a few back, plus more rocks . . . sharp ones.

It took most of the rest of the night to get everybody out of the canyon. And, I can't really remember much because I had a hard time staying awake. Mr. Murry made me get in his truck with the heater running, which pretty much did me in.

I do remember waking up when they got Dreggs to the top and he started throwing a fit that he and Ike had been hoodwinked by a couple of smart little rats.

"It's not right, Sheriff. I was defendin' myself," Dreggs kept explaining as they stuffed his giant body into the police car. I could tell everyone wanted to start laughing about that.

By the time they got James and Mr. Leland up, a couple of ambulances arrived, and I got to ride with James to the hospital. I tried to tell everyone that I was okay, but they stuffed me into a bed and I conked right out . . . probably from that white pill the nurse put in my mouth.

When I started to come out of my sleepy fog, I could make out Gram looking down at me, and sunlight streaming in the hospital window.

"Calvin? How ya feelin', Hon?"

I moved a little and it felt like someone had worked me over with a big stick.

"Fine, I guess. Sore." I figured I better make sure I wasn't feeling too good, just in case Uncle Neal was around. I needed him to feel a little sorry for me. I wasn't in the mood for a bedside lecture.

"I would expect so, Hon. Sounds like you all had quite the tumble." She patted my hand when she said that. Gram was a confirmed hand patter.

"James and Mr. Leland are here," she added. She could see that I wanted to ask something.

"James is banged up but going to be fine," she continued with a little smile. "And Mr. Leland, well, he's real banged up."

"But, he'll be okay, right?"

"I hope so," she said in her usual sweet voice. Gram was so nice, even when she had bad news. She could tell you that aliens had just attacked and flattened the whole town and you'd feel okay about it.

A lady about Gram's age poked her head in the door. "Mrs. Poag?" she said real soft. "May I come in?"

"Sure, Cal's awake now," Gram answered.

The little lady shuffled over and stood next to my bed. "I'm Alfred's wife, Maggie," she said. When she smiled at me, little tears leaked out the corners of her eyes, which just about made me want to cry too. "I want to thank you for what you did . . . for Alfred, I mean. I can't see yer friend yet, the Doctor won't let me. So, I just wanted to thank you."

She had my hand now and was squeezing it just a little. It felt warm and soft. It was also shaking just a little.

Gram put her arm around Mrs. Leland's shoulder and gave her a nice tight hug. Gram was like that with folks. She always knew when they needed something, and hugs were her specialty. Some grandmas make cookies, others cook like the army's gonna stop by. My Gram handed out hugs like candy on Halloween.

I had no idea what to say to Mrs. Leland. I would have done what I did even if Mr. Leland wasn't there, but I figured that wouldn't sound right somehow.

The fact was, James is the one she really needed to thank, because I learned later that he'd laid right next to Mr. Leland to keep him warm and gave him almost all the water. He was the hero. I just drove the car.

I kind of snickered whenever I thought about that—I'd just driven the car, like it was a bank heist or something.

Mrs. Leland shuffled back out of the room and Gram started feeding me something soft and fruity.

While I was still in the hospital, Uncle Neal brought in the Salmon and Hood River papers and showed me all the different stuff that'd been written up on us and those killers.

The police figured out real quick that Ike was Ike

Turello and Dreggs was actually Hank D. Walters, both wanted for robbing a Montana co-op and a string of other places I'd never heard of. The sheriff told me, when he came to visit, that James and me should feel pretty lucky. I did. James did too, I think. Later, when we finally got to be alone, he told me he'd been pretty scared when he heard Dreggs trying to get down into the canyon to finish off him and Mr. Leland.

I was only in the hospital for a day or so, but Gram brought me down to Salmon every day to visit James, who was in for a week. I even got to skip school a few days to rest and visit.

Even while propped up in his hospital bed and hurting in a hundred places, James wanted desperately to start working on "the story." We both knew it would be the best camping story for years to come and James wanted to make sure he had all the particulars straight in his mind for when summer rolled back around. He even told me, "Write this story down, Cal. We got to be accurate." I agreed to have a sleepover at his house as soon as he was better to test out a few of the parts.

"It won't be as good, sitting in my basement," he complained. "This story needs a good cracklin' campfire and lots of s'mores."

For James, setting the right mood was very important. Just writing it down on paper was good enough for me.

"If you got the right mood, ya know, with a good fire goin' and it's dark, and everyone huddled around, you can tell even a wimpy story and get kids scared 'n layin' awake in their sacks," he told me once after a crummy story that I admit got me kind of sweaty.

So, he knew that this story was going to make kids wet their pants. And the fact that it's true made it all the better.

I ended up telling the police about the wino I'd cross-blocked out the boxcar and it turned out he was in the same hospital as us. I didn't go visit him, though. I didn't think he'd understand, but I did ask Gram to take him some flowers. It was good to know I wasn't a killer.

"Tell him they're from an anonymous hobo," I said. She smiled and did it. Apparently, he asked her quietly if she could sneak him some Four Roses. I don't think she ever did, knowing her general opinion of winos and hobos.

◇ CHAPTER 14 ◇

Somewhat Cool and Humble Hero

After dodging all the stuff Dreggs and Ike had thrown at us, I started to worry that maybe I'd become cool. Of course, James and I were basically heroes and all the kids wanted to hear our stories . . . we got tons of attention. James really didn't need much more help being cool . . . he just was. For me, though, having kids come up and ask me to tell about this or that started to make me nervous. They were acting like I was cool, even some of the girls did too. They thought we were tough and brave and, well, cool. But me and James never really talked about it in those terms . . . we both knew we'd been scared out of our shorts most of the time.

Trying to make the whole thing "cool" meant that we'd had it all figured out and then set it in motion for the fun of it. Like we'd made up "The Do or Die Time" board game or something. Actually, we'd done some stupid stuff that boxed us into some scary places, and we were lucky we lived and those two rascals got caught.

I hadn't gotten a whipping like I'd been thinking I would the whole time. Gram even stepped in and put the clamps down on Uncle Neal the first time he tried to fillet me out for something else. That was something I really appreciated. Because, like I said, I knew we'd been stupid and anything Uncle Neal could have said would have been like telling a mouse that cats are dangerous.

But, when I'd hear James talk about the whole thing, it was like he'd stripped out all the scared-out-of-our-pants stuff and saw it like a movie or something.

He even started telling about my "great block" that saved his life. I guess he figured if I'd saved his life I wouldn't mind him telling that part of the story. Frankly, I didn't care. It'd been in the papers so everyone knew.

Grown men would come up to me in the store or someplace and fake a block and then laugh and slap me on the back.

* * *

James found me sitting alone on the edge of the Salmon River canyon. I'd started coming out there not long after getting back home. It was a cold November day. It had started to snow last night and the rocks were dusted like sugar.

"Look what I got," he said and handed me a little photo album. I flipped it open. "It's all the articles and stuff."

Sure enough, someone had collected everything that talked about our adventure.

"Where'd you get this?" I was interested, of course, but there was this part of me that wasn't ready to walk back through all the events. James was. Like I said, he was ready to write a book or something. He just didn't know how to write.

He told me not long after getting home that I should write a book because I knew how to spell and stuff.

"Yeah, that'd help," I said half-heartedly. Write a book. Brother. Who'd want to read about two stupid kids getting nabbed by a couple of stupider criminals?

I thanked him for the album and got up to leave. I knew he'd been the one to put it together. He never wanted to forget any detail.

"Where ya goin'?" he asked. "Let's go build a fire in the cave and hang out for a while."

"Nah, I got homework."

Really, I didn't want to sit around saying things like, "Boy, wasn't it cool when Dreggs was gonna blow our heads off?" Or, "that truck sure flew through the air, didn't it?" And then laugh like it was an amazing ride at the county fair. It just didn't work for me.

Without really knowing it, I started just going off by myself and doing things on my own. I even went back to the spot where we'd found Jenkins and just sat there for a while.

After they pulled his body from Mud Lake, I wasn't scared to swim there. And even if they hadn't dragged his creepy body ashore, I think I might have gone swimming there.

Both James and me had to be there to identify the body, and that was pretty hard. By then, he looked like a man-shaped prune.

One of Sheriff Stubbs' deputies ran off into the bushes and barfed his guts out and we just looked at each other and smiled. Harold was still working his magic on folks. We just weren't getting any money for it!

The whole thing hardened up some stuff in me . . . some baby stuff that I later discovered needed to go anyway. Funny thing is it didn't seem to really affect James all that much. As always, he took things in stride and just moved on. It all ended up in his sack of stories that he dragged out every chance he got to make someone's eyes pop out.

James was still my best friend, though, and would be for a long time. You won't be surprised to hear that about all my broken bones and permanent scars, James was there, pushing me beyond what I thought was sane or safe. My body was a living road map of all the things we had done.

A few years later, on a camping trip, we started talking and looking back at that time with Dreggs and Ike, and that was the first time I really wanted to recount our adventure and was able to laugh about it.

"Do or Die Time," James said slow and mysterious. "That's a great name for a book."

I just smiled back. "Yeah."

I don't know about James, but, for me, laughing that night about those couple of days was really about my fears and sheer dumb luck. It wasn't about being cool, but we must have had some grit to make it through that adventure.

Do or die time? Maybe, I thought. I decided to let it work around in my head for a while.

◇ CHAPTER 15 ◇

A Taste of Heaven

My new fly rod was bent so far I thought for sure it would break. Then, when that lunker jumped, he was at least twenty inches and probably four pounds; the kind of challenge I was lookin' for with my one-pound test. Light line and big fish was one of the things that changed soon after I got home and healed up. The better I got with dry flies, the lighter the line I used, and the smaller the flies.

It took all my new skills to not jerk and be impatient. I let him run, I reeled in, I played him gently, and stole back some more line. Finally, the net reached in and I had him!

"That's a beaut, Calvin," Alfred complimented. "I think I caught this old boy last time I was in here," he went on while looking at the large fish in his net. He should know; he'd been fishing the Salmon River for fifty years.

"Ya gonna keep 'im?" he asked.

I thought about it a second. "Nope, let's see if you can catch him again. Half a sandwich says you can't. Ya got fifteen minutes," I declared my bet.

"What kind of sandwich ya got, kid?"

"Spam. With American cheese," I said, like it was the best thing in the world.

"Ummm. Let 'im go. I believe I could eat another half a sandwich." There was a sly smile at the corners of his mouth. "I'm prayin' first."

"Prayin? To catch a fish?"

"No, I'm sayin' grace for that sandwich I'm about to win!" Alfred laughed and starting switching flies.

The End

The Authors

Cameron Ventura has been telling visual stories for a long time. His career as a filmmaker has provided him the opportunity to tell many types of stories. He's also a creator in other mediums, plays the guitar, and lives on a small farm with his wife of thirty-plus years, Linda.

Cameron has written several other Calvin Poag adventures, soon to be released by Hidden Shelf Publishing House. Follow him at www.CameronVentura.com.

Dennis Mansfield has long been a passionate man of progress, from his time at West Point to a bid for the U.S. Congress. When he and his wife's beloved son, Nate, passed away suddenly, Dennis changed his life's course from personal ambition to helping others. "You might say that it sharpened my perspective and gave me clarity about what is truly important." Whether coaching business executives, speaking at an event, or writing a book, Dennis has focused on imparting courage to others, helping them overcome challenges that might hamper success . . . in business, in relationships, in life.

Dennis and his wife, Susan, have enjoyed traveling the world together, but they're happiest riding bikes along the Boise River greenbelt . . . and being with their children and grandchildren.

Follow him at www.DennisMansfield.com.

Acknowledgments

Cameron

For the most part, writing is a solitary endeavor, but many have offered a hand. My wife, Linda, who's been my honest sounding board. Dennis, your influence and contribution to my life can never be overstated. Leslie Bair, your early read was the encouragement needed to keep going. Elaine Foxall and the other English teachers and students who critiqued *Do or Die Time* in the early stages. Kathy Gaudry and Bob Gaines, for jumping in and running your insightful comb through the tangles. Scott Ziemer, you have no idea how much you've encouraged me over thirty years of our friendship. Kiri Zooper, your laser direction. My grandparents for their childhood wonderland in Trout Lake, Washington. And, of course, God! Thanks for letting me do something I love.

Dennis

Many thanks to Cameron for our decades of friendship, mutual belief in Christianity, appreciation of story, and love of film. Thanks to Linda Ventura and Susan Mansfield for teaching young adults to love reading, stories, and teachers. And also, thanks to Linda and Susan for loving their wild husbands. Thanks to my five young adventurers—Nathan, Megan, Colin, Cole, and Amelia—for our stories together.